GW01403401

REVIVAL!

WE HAVE IGNITION!

REVIVAL!

WE HAVE IGNITION!

MINDY SAVOIA

XULON PRESS

Xulon Press
555 Winderley Pl, Suite 225
Maitland, FL 32751
407.339.4217
www.xulonpress.com

xulon PRESS

© 2024 by Mindy Savoia

All rights reserved solely by the author. The author guarantees all contents
are original and do not infringe upon the legal rights of any other person
or work. No part of this book may be reproduced in any form without the
permission of the author.

Due to the changing nature of the Internet, if there are any web addresses,
links, or URLs included in this manuscript, these may have been altered
and may no longer be accessible. The views and opinions shared in this
book belong solely to the author and do not necessarily reflect those of the
publisher. The publisher therefore disclaims responsibility for the views or
opinions expressed within the work.

Unless otherwise indicated, Scripture quotations taken from the Revised
Standard Version (RSV). Copyright © 1946, 1952, and 1971 the Division of
Christian Education of the National Council of the Churches of Christ in the
United States of America. Used by permission. All rights reserved.

Paperback ISBN-13: 979-8-86850-399-3
Ebook ISBN-13: 979-8-86850-400-6

REVIVAL!

WE HAVE IGNITION!

MINDY SAVOIA

XULON PRESS

Xulon Press
555 Winderley Pl, Suite 225
Maitland, FL 32751
407.339.4217
www.xulonpress.com

xulon PRESS

© 2024 by Mindy Savoia

All rights reserved solely by the author. The author guarantees all contents
are original and do not infringe upon the legal rights of any other person
or work. No part of this book may be reproduced in any form without the
permission of the author.

Due to the changing nature of the Internet, if there are any web addresses,
links, or URLs included in this manuscript, these may have been altered
and may no longer be accessible. The views and opinions shared in this
book belong solely to the author and do not necessarily reflect those of the
publisher. The publisher therefore disclaims responsibility for the views or
opinions expressed within the work.

Unless otherwise indicated, Scripture quotations taken from the Revised
Standard Version (RSV). Copyright © 1946, 1952, and 1971 the Division of
Christian Education of the National Council of the Churches of Christ in the
United States of America. Used by permission. All rights reserved.

Paperback ISBN-13: 979-8-86850-399-3
Ebook ISBN-13: 979-8-86850-400-6

Books by Mindy Savoia

Ride into Life

Ride into Life: The Legacy

The Gallery: An Allegorical Journey

Missed Gifts of the Holy Spirit

REVIVAL! We Have Ignition!

DEDICATION

Dedicated to the life, memory, and work of Carrie Norlin,
a master educator who excelled in teaching others to love
what they care about and to care for what they love.

ACKNOWLEDGMENTS

Graham, thank you for your input; you are an unwavering
hero to many.
Steve, your limitless support parallels your limitless love.
Michael, thank you for your IT guidance. You make it look easy.
Nicole, you are the best daughter-in-law anyone could ask for.
Pam and Gabe, you are real-deal Christians.
My grandchildren, you are my treasures!
My God, my all!

A new heart I will give you, and a new spirit I will put within you; and I will take out of your flesh the heart of stone and give you a heart of flesh. (Ezekiel 36:26)

TABLE OF CONTENTS

INTRODUCTION

The world was a different place, very different. That was before the Lord's great revival and the harvest of hearts and souls. Many traveled to new locations because they felt nudged. Some noticed, yet many did not know, did not recognize it, at least not at first. The small, yet strong group was larger than in the past. The past included the Old Testament, the New Testament, and encompassed revivals throughout the centuries both within and outside the Americas. Imagine a world map and the spread of a fierce contagion. Now picture that same world map, saturated with a great healing, a promise, and the truth ablaze, all activated by an outpouring of the Spirit of God.

This novel had already been set in motion for a number of years. The author credits ideas for segments of the work from a series of her own dreams that spanned from 2020 – 2021. They occurred before modern-day college campus revivals began to radiate. We are on the cusp of a momentous harvest of souls that will stem from the youth and transition many of us into an awesome future.

CHAPTER ONE
DON'T GET ME STARTED

"I should have been part of that crew. I knew they were going to select me; well, that was before."

"Go on, and please take your time," the doctor encouraged.

The older woman chuckled, "At my age, I don't know how much time I have."

The therapist smiled and nodded, "Just say whatever is on your heart, Ruby."

A few moments passed and then, "It was wrong, wrong that Daddy died, just days after those poor astronauts," the client's cadence broke.

"Ruby, what was wrong about his passing?"

After a lengthy pause, "He died. Anyway, I should have gone on ahead of him; you know, with the team."

"What might that have changed?" the mental health professional gently urged.

Ruby quickly inserted, "Can we talk about something else for the rest of today's session?"

"We can, but I believe you have arrived at an important place."

"Doctor, what will we really resolve? It was so many, many years ago."

"What keeps bringing you here to see me, Ruby?"

"Not what, but who—my granddaughter. She wants me to have peace." The old woman stared momentarily at the therapist and then shifted her focus toward a window. "There will be plenty of time for peace when I'm gone."

"Ruby, why do you believe your granddaughter wants you to have peace?"

She chuckled and simultaneously shook her head. Then the woman returned her eyes to the doctor's face, "So that I'll stop getting on her case."

"Getting on her case about what?"

Ruby pushed back, "That might be best to discuss during our next appointment."

The younger woman glanced at the clock on the wall of her office. "Ruby, please consider this. From what you've shared, I am sure your grandchild loves you very much." The elderly woman sat slightly hunched and gazed at the counselor, shrugging her shoulders at the same time that the corners of her mouth sagged downward. The therapist continued, "How old did you say the baby was when she came to live with you and your husband?"

"Right from the hospital," Ruby offered.

Both women acknowledged the end of the session for that day. The therapist stood, which was a signal that Ruby should do the same. The patient liked the psychologist from the start. She was middle-aged, attractive, and African American. The two hit it off from their first dialogue when they discovered they were both originally from Florida. Although Ruby was of a European-American lineage, her husband's mother had been Black. Ruby studied the therapist's face. The patient suddenly missed the family matriarch and recalled how much she loved the rich accounts of life that her mother-in-law shared over the years.

Dr. Davis walked around the desk and evenly offered, "I'll see you in a week, Ruby. Please jot down any thoughts in your journal that relate to how you felt when your grandbaby moved in." The doctor opened the door for her client, who had collected purse and cane before rising. The elder lady smiled and slowly blinked as if she wanted to say something but then walked out of the office.

⚬⚬⚬⚬⚬

Evangeline stepped out from the car, backpack over one shoulder and two grocery bags in the other hand. The smell of fresh-cut grass illuminated memories of a carefree childhood and sweet new growth. But now, it was time for her to help. "It's okay, Grams; I've got this."

"Thanks, E.V. These old joints surely appreciate you." Ruby's eyes twinkled as she pried herself loose from the vehicle's driver seat with a grunt. She pulled her purse onto one arm and then reached for and situated the cane, a recent addition, underneath her weight. "I still cannot believe that now I'm using this to help me walk. Should've taken more notice when the eye doctor added bifocals to my reading glasses. Since Grandpa Bill passed, it seems like I've been going downhill."

"You're still young, Grams, just lonely."

Ruby laughed. "I could never be lonely with you, sweet child ..."

The two stepped into the house, and E.V. grinned as she completed her grandmother's sentence, "... or bored." They both snickered. E.V. set the grocery bags on the counter, opened the refrigerator, and reached for a bottle of sweet tea. The teenager twisted off the cap.

"Wash your hands first, girl."

"Grams, the pandemic is over," she sighed. Whether from habit or for the sake of indulging the aging woman, the youth moved toward the sink. As the water ran, E.V. thought about how nice she had imagined it would be to get back to real classes for her senior year in high school, where students and teachers were together, in person, as opposed to online learning from remote sites. She shook her head to reaffirm just how useless the majority of her peer group was. That was a sad guarantee, she thought. "I'll be in my room, Grams. I have homework for my government class, you know, U.S. Constitution and old stuff to memorize."

"Gonna do it, Eves?"

"Don't know, Grams." With a flick of her head, she pulled a cell phone from a torn back pocket in her most comfortable, shredded jeans. E.V. made her way down the hallway and stopped at the first bedroom. The girl entered, shut the door, and flopped down on the bed to check her messages. She rolled over and was prompted to pull her history notebook out of the worn backpack on the floor. She looked down at the greyed satchel and momentarily relived a happy memory of her excitement when years before, she got that new bookbag.

E.V. enjoyed history just like her Grandpa Bill did. They had often discussed wars, what led up to them, and changes in the United States and other countries after the conflicts had ended. He would often tell her, "History repeats itself and will keep being repeated until folks learn from it."

She wondered how those early writers of the U.S. Constitution had sorted it all out. Sure, they might have had different clothing, wigs, and lifestyles, yet something about those days always intrigued E.V. Her peers would argue with teachers that the original rules of the country no more applied to the present than a song from the 1940s could interest modern-day music fans.

E.V. suddenly cringed at a flashback. Her own voice replayed over and over again in her head like a scratched vinyl album on the outdated stereo record player her grandparents cherished. "I don't agree," she leaned over and whispered to a classmate on that day. "I still like listening to oldies." The other student shrugged, and E.V. berated herself for sharing something so trivial, yet at the same time, so revealing about her personal life. She shook her head, along with the memories that held on like unwanted emotional attachments.

Ruby and Bill insisted that their granddaughter start piano lessons by the age of five. "The melody unlocks parts of your brain while your hands are working other parts," Grandpa Bill would say. By third grade, E.V. begged to add fiddle lessons after watching a country music show with her grandparents. Thus, violin instruction expanded her repertoire. E.V. also had a lovely voice by her family's standards, but she was never convinced about that.

Both grandparents had been educators before they retired. Grams taught junior high science, and G-pa Bill was a high school history teacher. A well-rounded education had been important to E.V.'s guardians. Bill had served in the armed forces and then studied education. He said a teaching career allowed him to continue serving his country.

E.V. once played kickball, rode her bicycle, and jumped rope. All that changed in fourth grade. Fifth grade was lonely. Sixth grade was a complete aberration. Junior high was torture. Memories abounded.

E.V. forced herself to return to the post-pandemic present. She opened the notebook. At least, she had her artwork. Every available space inside both covers of the spiral-bound treasure represented pieces of her. She showed very little on the outside of the booklet. However, her personal world was well characterized within both, front and back covers. E.V. used a fingernail to trace the lines of one of her own illustrations that started as half a rainbow before the first page of writing. She flipped to the last page of the notebook. What the talented teen had begun, traditionally broadcast by the use of colorful pens and pencils, took on different hues within the sketch. The remaining arc of the rainbow was continued inside the back cover. It had been completed with black pen and ink hatching and cross hatching where the intensity of tones was varied as a stark contrast. She worked the second half of the drawing after Bill Gold died.

The day G-pa Bill passed, it began to rain and seemed to rain for days and days. When E.V. sighed and complained about it, Grams reminded her that Florida always received lots of moisture. The sun finally broke through as they walked back to the car after the graveside service. E.V. felt a sense of peace and hope when she looked up and took in a rainbow, framed by some of the large oak trees that surrounded the cemetery. Her grandfather had taught her long before, on a fishing excursion, that Florida was home to live oaks. She nodded and smiled to herself that a tree with such a name was planted in great numbers throughout and around the burial grounds.

Evangeline leaned over the edge of her bed and drew out a box that was stored below. She opened it and with great satisfaction, pulled out a collection of her favorite drawings from throughout her childhood. The illustrations included colorful musical notations on lined staffs with doodles of small animal caricatures that stood out from the tinted spaces and lines. E.V. smiled as she looked through renditions of the family pets, created by her application of pencils, crayons, and markers. There were also photographs of horses. How she loved to ride! Equestrian lessons began when she was eight and were a relished part of her life.

E.V. perused the contents of that special box. She lifted up an old photo of Uncle Brad and herself standing in front of his motorcycle. She was struck by how small she was, not that long ago. Back on that particular day, highlighted in the glossy photo, she enjoyed a special trip with her uncle on his chopper. Reminiscing, E.V. reflected that they probably just drove through the neighborhood, but as a child, she was sure it had been a much more exciting adventure.

According to Grams, the girl loved it too much. Ruby was concerned that her granddaughter would want to learn how to ride and then, someday own her own bike. E.V. remembered when G-pa Bill laughed, "Sure, the woman who wanted to fly around in space worries about a motorcycle!"

As E.V. pored over the photographs and drawings in her cherished treasure box, it was as though she watched a movie trailer that pieced together clips of her life. The initial day of fourth grade began much like any other first day of school. Equipped with new school supplies, a contemporary outfit, and unsoiled shoes, E.V. announced to her grandparents that she knew where her class was located.

When Grams and G-pa offered to walk the girl inside on that bright morning, E.V. broadcast, "I'm a fourth grader, not a little kid anymore!" Resigned to the girl's strong will, Ruby and Bill dropped her off in front of the school and nodded as E.V. exited. She made her grandparents promise that she would be allowed to take the school bus thereafter. The elementary student turned away with a quick wave as soon as she shut the rear passenger-side door of the old blue sedan.

E.V. checked the number on the classroom door and felt quite grown up. She made sure her new outfit, shoes, and backpack were set just right. At that moment, Evangeline Gold stepped out of her past and into the future. School work was deemed easy enough by the almost nine-year-old. During break, she had a difficult time connecting with some of the new students. Kristopher and Lisa were in her classes since kindergarten. The three had been inseparable in school. They sat together that first day of the new academic year during lunch as had been their past ritual. The young man was quiet. When the class was dismissed outdoors for recess, Kris shouted, "See ya!" and ran off to choose sides with two teams of boys.

Lisa, dressed in a new matching set of shorts and top, inched closer to E.V. Her red-braided pigtails swished back and forth as she shook her head, "Wow, it's like he doesn't even know us anymore!" They both shrugged and decided to join some girls who were drawing chalk hopscotch boards on the blacktop.

The biggest girl in the group had one hand on her hip as she instructed the others to pick their own marker rocks. "We'll use my board, since it's the best one." When Lisa and E.V. approached, the ringleader rolled her eyes and motioned to the others with a tilt of her head. She looked toward the intruders, "We already have six players."

"Any number can play," Lisa defied. Her pigtails whooshed with added emphasis.

E.V. raised her eyebrows and tipped her head toward Lisa. "Eight might be the perfect number for a new round," she asserted. The two newcomers moved in. The others did not appear amused. Once the game began, the females seemed to get along, yet E.V. was not convinced about their motives. At least I still have Lisa, she silently assured herself.

According to E.V., the day only became worse, The teacher did not choose E.V. when her hand shot up multiple times. However, the single question E.V. was unsure of in social studies that afternoon was the one the teacher requested she answer. "I don't know, Miss Salter. Why didn't you call on me earlier, and how come we aren't learning real history?" The girl felt her face redden and heat up when she heard snickers rustle around the room.

That night during supper, both grandparents took turns asking school questions with eager anticipation. E.V. sounded indifferent. G-pa finally probed, "Is everything okay, honey?"

The fourth grader announced, "I'd like to go to my room, please."

The older couple eyed one another and nodded. Ruby reached for her granddaughter's arm as the girl pushed away and slid back the wooden captain's chair from the colonial-style circular dining table in a matching dark wood. "We're here if you'd like to talk, E.V." The fourth grader stood and cast her tear-brimmed eyes downward, sniffed once, and turned to walk into the bedroom hallway. After a silent pause, Ruby lowered her voice, "What'd you make of that, Bill?"

He lifted a forkful of meatloaf and mashed potatoes after pushing some green peas on top of the mix, "Kids are weird, and they become even stranger as adults."

"That's the truth," Ruby answered. She used her thumb to trace the designs etched in a crystal water pitcher that sat on the table as she silently pondered why neither Bonnie nor Bradley ever struggled socially. E.V. heard every word, spoken and unspoken.

"Enough memories," E.V. whispered aloud to convince herself. "I need to study." With that, Evangeline placed the cover back on top of her keepsake box and lowered it to the floor. With a slight motion of the back of her foot, she tucked the case and its memories under the bed.

E.V. woke before dawn. Disoriented, she wondered whether she had just had a nightmare. She was a young adult in the dream and walked through an old but clean and well-kept city. There were ongoing ceremonies that celebrated groundbreakings and fresh innovations.

Evangeline replayed parts of the dream in her head. A young woman, slightly older than E.V. in the dream, stepped out of a building and onto the sidewalk. She had bright eyes and a beautiful smile. Her skin tone was a smooth mixture of tans and caramels. To E.V., her lineage appeared to be a blended composition from many cultures. The woman explained that she changed her direction in life and asked whether Evangeline was disappointed in her. E.V. replied, "No." E.V. did not recognize her but thought she should have. The two walked together. Many people crossed the street at the four-way, perpendicular corners. E.V. and the woman walked to the right while others went straight. Only a few skewed to the left. Those moving straight through the crosswalk had to negotiate potholes.

The two arrived at a tiny, treeless park that held two concrete benches set into walls with buildings all around. Both females sat across from a young man with light skin, dark frizzy, wild hair, and thick-rimmed glasses. He sat next to another young woman who said her name meant strong, gentle worker and introduced the male as one who rules peacefully.

A handsome teen who wore an oversized wooden cross on a leather cord was sprinting toward them and then stopped. Another boy followed and paused with the one who was running. The first, pointed toward a bridge over a waterway a few miles away. Jesus Christ stood, larger than life, upon and towered over the top of the bridge. Burning, heavy debris fell all around, but the six were protected.

Chapter Two

DRIVEN TO KNOW

The dream clung to E.V. throughout the next day. She walked past an open doorway during night school. Driver's Education class suddenly needed to be taken outside of daytime school hours. After pandemic funding had been exhausted, the district's slashed budget would no longer pay for such coursework. The Driver's Ed. curriculum was shifted from being classified as a high school elective to extracurricular. Publicly-funded schools lost students to both, the homeschool environment and small private academies. That equated to even further decreased revenue being allocated to districts. Certified teachers willing to volunteer were offered incentives such as continuing credit hours for their additional work, which included reporting and records management. It was a creative, inexpensive way to encourage educators to help juniors and seniors catch up on instruction missed during the time when schools were shuttered.

Ruby insisted someone, other than herself, would need to be responsible for E.V.'s training and practice. That individual should have been Bill, she reflected. Ruby neither trusted Bradley's commitment nor his practice of safety rules. Plus, the guardian requested the school issue a certificate of completion that could be recognized by her car insurance company, so E.V. would be eligible for a student discount.

E.V. stood up to stretch her legs and intended to take a short break. She signed out on the printed class roster next to: Gold, Evangeline

– Grade 12. The teen walked down a long hallway and past an open door with a sandwich board propped outside the room that announced, Christian Ministry Club. An adult male voice reached her ears, "... God came to earth as our Savior, cloaked as an ordinary human. With the exception of his family, Jesus was unknown to most mortals for the first three decades of his human life." The pause from within the space was unquenchable. "Then, Jesus' own mother gave him a nod during the wedding at Cana. It was time, and time would not stand still. The appropriate moment to go public and be made known had been revealed. There would be no turning back. What good could possibly come from Nazareth? By the way," the voice proclaimed, "that comes from John 1:46. So, Jesus moved forward through the universe to teach, heal, suffer, die, and rise that we might all have eternal life. You need only agree, ask him into your own heart, and then, promise to remain close to his."

E.V. slowed her gait, stepped back, and felt herself bend toward the doorway. She suddenly took account of her stance and straightened her spine. What was going on in there? The girl pondered and then figuratively shrugged it off as she resumed her trip to the restroom. E.V. rationalized that anything was less boring than Driver's Ed. 101 with its distances, brake times, and speed zones. She subconsciously rolled her eyes and wondered why the course was numbered when there was only one level offered at school.

Yet, E.V. weighed and measured what had been broadcast from the classroom she just walked by. E.V. had never heard such an intriguing point of view during the church services she attended with Grams and for years, G-pa Bill. She stopped and glanced at a large notice affixed to the wall. It was a colorful, hand-painted poster that invited students to pray at the flagpole by a pupil-led group every morning before first period. Hmm, she thought and struggled to recall. I don't remember ever seeing that before, she assured herself.

The teenager reached for the lavatory door handle. From a few classrooms away, E.V. could still hear the man's voice, "And in the

Gospel of Mark, Jesus looked upon the rich man with love and said to him, 'Come, follow me,' just as he invited others, as documented in Matthew and Luke. All that poor, wealthy man had to do first was sell all he had and give it to the needy."

E.V. physically stopped to listen but only for a moment. "Come, follow me." It was not the same voice that flowed from the man who preached from the classroom she had just moved ahead of. The tone was audible but not in her ears. The voice resonated deeper within her. She continued to walk. Upon exiting the girls' room, E.V. decided to take the longer way around and avoid the intriguing room altogether.

"Excuse me, Miss Gold."

Suddenly startled, E.V. spun around more quickly than she wished she had. She studied the eyes of the night school administrator and was sure that the woman recognized guilt. "Oh, hello, Ms. Devonshire."

"I believe the Driver's Ed. classroom is just a few doors back from the direction you were just heading."

"Oh, uh, yes, right, but you see," she swallowed, "I needed to stretch my legs."

"Thank you, Evangeline. Your certificate of completion is partially based on seat time. Please head directly to class."

There was no reason to argue. E.V. submitted a quick, "Okay." She promptly changed direction to return to the Driver's Ed. room via the shorter route. The teen felt the eyes of the woman remain locked onto her back.

As she once again approached the odd meeting room, E.V. heard, "Next week, we'll cover angel armies. Tonight, let's pray that Christ will surround each of us with examples of individuals who do his work, and that we too, may do his work. Then, we'll close with worship before our final prayer."

A young man with a guitar strapped over his shoulder came to the doorway, nodded at E.V., and quietly informed her, "We don't want to interrupt the other classes." He smiled and shut the door. E.V. took a step, then turned to check for Ms. Devonshire, but she was gone.

Each week, for the remaining half of the semester, E.V. dared to walk past that interesting room during her Driver's Ed. class time. Each week, she felt an uptick in her interest and a tug on her heart. And each week, she wondered.

After class, on that first night, Ruby was waiting for E.V. in the parking lot. "How was class, Eves?"

"Fine."

"That good?" Ruby quickly inserted.

The girl could not see her grandmother's full expression inside the dark vehicle, but she knew the woman was grinning. With a slight nod, E.V. smiled, close-lipped, "You know," she wrinkled her nose, "boring."

"Well, it won't be boring once you have your driver's license, dear."

"Truth!" E.V. sounded unusually animated.

Ruby pursued, "So, how do you intend to save up for a vehicle and pay for fuel and insurance?"

E.V. giggled and then became serious, "I was hoping to get a job and then use some of what you and G-pa Bill set aside for me. And I still have monthly benefits from Bonnie."

"G-pa and I intended for you to use the money in savings for education after high school. I suppose if you start at the local community college, you could have a vehicle stipend. A job sounds good, Eves. Your mother didn't exactly pay much into the government. One could say that her work record was not staggering. Plus, those survivor benefits will dry up soon. But remember, the Good Lord always provides," Ruby sighed.

E.V. thought for a moment and wondered whether to share with her grandmother what she experienced earlier that evening. "Grams?"

"Hmm?" The driver flipped on the windshield wipers as a light rain began to sprinkle.

"Does the Bible say we are to ask Jesus into our own hearts?"

"Good question, E.V. I'm no expert but do not recall ever reading that phrase. Maybe it would be something to ask the pastor on Sunday."

"Maybe," she paused, "never mind, but thanks." She peered out her side passenger window and into the darkness.

"I believe we should pray for increasing faith and trust," added Grams.

E.V. was clearly done discussing the topic. "What kind of car should I look for?"

The woman knew her granddaughter well. "Once you successfully complete the course, pass your driving test, and find a job, what would be your preference?"

"Old and comfortable," the teen nodded as the two pulled into the driveway, "like my jeans."

E.V. helped Ruby out of the car. Once inside, Grams decided to have a steaming cup of tea while E.V. helped herself to freshly baked cookies in a container on the counter. As was tradition, they hugged and wished each other a good night's rest.

Ruby remained at the kitchen table and leafed through the newspaper from earlier in the day. She sipped her tea and mulled over E.V.'s response about an old, comfortable car. That was classic Evangeline, but only to those who knew her well. To the rest of the world, she was an artistic introvert who preferred to wear dark clothing and bold makeup accents. After the epidemic, the teen added subtle highlights of blue, green, and purple to her hair. When the girl did speak, her clever quips often rang on the side of sarcasm.

Ruby reminisced back to when E.V. was in eighth grade. She had been called to pick her granddaughter up from school for using an expletive in English class, which resulted in an off-campus suspension. On the quiet ride home, Ruby finally asked, "E.V., what were you trying to prove? I know the swear word did not simply slip out."

Looking straight ahead and through the windshield from the passenger side, she breathed with resignation, "Words, Grams, not word."

"E.V., the vice principal only mentioned one unacceptable four-letter word."

"Yup, but I demonstrated how it could be used as a noun, verb, adjective, and an interjection," E.V. stated with detached dryness.

Grams always said the girl was savvy and very lucky that she was raised by two older adults who were a bit tired and worn. Ruby decided to pick her battles and only hesitantly approved of her grandchild's choices in wearing dark clothing. She eventually yielded to E.V. dyeing black, that which Ruby referred to as her granddaughter's beautiful, natural strawberry-blonde hair. That decision led to other colors and styles, but Ruby drew the line at facial piercings and tattoos. Evangeline had usually respected the boundaries set by her grandparents.

The woman's mind bobbed upon ripples of memories. Her daughter, Bonnie, seemed to have had endless friends and acquaintances. Nevertheless, the few who showed up at Bonnie's funeral provided an unspoken reality to the grief-stricken mother. As teens, they we more interested in cutting classes, trying gateway drugs, and concocting elaborate lies. More times than not, Ruby would fuss that telling the truth required far less energy expenditure. As young adults, they either turned away from their juvenile immaturity or remained in the same quicksand that swallowed up Bonnie.

Where was E.V. in that model? Ruby pondered with anxious trepidation. Lisa had been E.V.'s only other close friend. E.V. and Kristopher kept in contact during the summer he moved away. Lisa still lived in the area, and she and E.V. attended the same school. In the past, the girls shared thoughts and experiences. While Lisa was attracted to what Grams called pretty clothes, pink and pastel-colored nail polish, and dance classes, E.V.'s attire became darker. She enjoyed nail polish as well, yet moved from blues to deep purple shades. Ruby was uncomfortable with the motivation for the black nail polish E.V. came home wearing after a shopping trip with Lisa. The granddaughter insisted that she had used her own money for the purchase and liked the way it looked. Ruby also knew that Lisa had once accepted E.V. as creative, intelligent, and someone she could trust. Nevertheless, by the second half of high school, Lisa appeared to lean toward a different set of friends. E.V. also met some new acquaintances at the larger school. Ruby heard about Scarlett, Emma, and Destiny but only as names.

E.V. returned to the kitchen, "Grams?"

The woman looked up from where she sat at the kitchen table. She didn't seem to be startled but slowly came back to the present. "What is it, Eves?"

"I called you twice from the hallway. Are you okay?"

"Sure, child. Had just been revisiting some memories."

"Was it about Challenger, again?"

The older lady chuckled, "No, Eves, not this time." Ruby stood up. She needed to shake off her gnawing unanswered questions. "I thought you went to bed."

"Well, I did, Grams, but then had a feeling you needed to ask me something."

The woman began where her thoughts left off. "Do you have friends at school, Eves?"

Evangeline looked up toward the ceiling and then, her eyes met those of the grandmother, "Kind of."

Ruby sighed, "E.V., your teachers have said you barely talk in class, yet you always shared so much with Grandpa Bill and I."

E.V. responded, "That's because G-pa always said I was witty," she slyly smiled, "and you've always needed me to talk, Grams."

"Goodnight, and sleep well, child."

E.V. kissed the still-soft cheek of the only maternal guardian she had ever truly known, "You too, Grams."

The girl walked back to her room and climbed into bed. She knew; she just knew that her grandmother needed to talk. "Hmm," she murmured and turned out the light.

CHAPTER THREE

READY OR NOT

"I'm telling you; she's a witch!" Kelly stomped her foot.

Becca tried to be the peacemaker, "Oh, leave her alone." E.V. looked upward, then down slightly, and sighed.

Meagan just couldn't let it go. She faked concern with the shake of her head and a dramatic counterfeit pout, "Tell us again how your poor cat died, Kelly."

Kelly's lower lip quivered, and she spoke with heavy caution, "We found him near our yard with a dead toad nearby." She pointed at E.V. Her voice rose in tempo and volume, "E.V. yelled at the teacher the day before about the cruelty of frog dissections! Then, she turned to glare at me with that, that look! I knew it! I just knew she hated me!"

E.V. briefly shut her eyes and wished that she could actually make them all disappear. Blinking twice, she looked squarely at Kelly and lowered her voice, "Then you'd better get out of my way before I turn you into something worse than you already are." The three girls parted along the sidewalk, and E.V. moved through the center of the walkway as if she owned it. She couldn't believe that was all it took, although she assured herself it meant future retaliation unless she maintained the upper hand.

After the verbal altercation, E.V. just wanted to get home and move straight to her chores. She walked from the bus stop and muttered under her breath, "Brood of vipers." E.V. dared not turn around.

She listened for the sound of footsteps to the rear, but there weren't any. Expected whispers called out in silence.

The door slammed shut behind the preteen, and Ruby called out, "E.V.?"

The girl raised her voice, "In the laundry room."

"Wow, you sure are motivated on a Friday afternoon, dear!" Ruby realized she was shouting and lowered her voice as she neared the utility room.

The girl did not demonstrate a marked emotional response, "Just getting to the inevitable." E.V.'s grandparents had always assigned responsibilities and household tasks to her, even as a young child. E.V. clearly understood why. No one could make the mistake of calling either guardian or the youngest family member, spoiled. They all worked hard for what they had earned, including Evangeline. When she wanted a small aquarium, a rabbit, and chickens, E.V. had to save her money to buy the animals and then, worked off the necessary expenses to cover their food and living quarters. She knew that her grandparents meant it when they said there would only be one warning to feed, clean up after, or provide attention to her pets. A strict schedule was always attached to the refrigerator with magnets.

The older married couple often wondered and were open about whether their past, laid-back approach to parenting played into unhealthy factors. Those influences may have led to the demise of their daughter, Bonnie, and then attributed to what they defined as laziness in her brother, Bradley. Ruby and Bill never hid that from Evangeline. The youngster did not often think about Bonnie, her own mother. After all, the toddler was barely three when the woman overdosed. Uncle Brad was always fun but didn't stop by very often.

Of course, there were times when E.V. observed other children with their moms and secretly wished she had such a persona in her life. Then, there were the remaining instances, and E.V. was relieved she did not have the obligation. Besides, she reasoned that Ruby and Bill loved their granddaughter and truly were very good to her.

E.V. shook herself out of the daydreams and back to the current moment. She mentally regrouped after the loathsome memories. She was seated in the high school cafeteria when she looked up from her food. There they were, the same trio in present time, across from her on the opposite side of the lunch room: the fat one, the skinny one, and the one with so much acne, E.V. almost felt sorry for her. She couldn't even remember which one was called Meagan, or the name of the one E.V. referred to as the toad, or fungi, or whatever the third's name was. E.V. caught herself murmuring, "A huddle of toadstools," under her breath. Yes, she thought with a nod. That term did fit them quite well. She imagined that her grandmother would have suggested there were nicer ways to describe people if one were to designate titles for others at all. In fact, she was sure that Grams would have delivered a mini lecture about not judging. Period. E.V. gently shook her head with a convinced sideways smile that there just weren't any polite variations for what she was thinking.

A group of four students approached the table where E.V. was sitting while she ate. Two were dressed in comparatively similar styles to E.V.'s clothing. When the school reopened after the shutdown, its dress code was seen as out-of-date. Policies fell short of covering all the new hairstyles, piercings, and tattoos. Schools couldn't afford the loss of students that would ensue. Therefore, dress codes and handbooks were modified. Ruby had asked E.V. how kids could have possibly shopped when everything was shut down.

E.V.'s flippant response was truthful, "Determination finds a way, Grams."

Two girls and two boys neared E.V. in the lunchroom. She sat by herself. The female, who led the way, introduced herself as Millie. She quickly spouted the names of the others, Callista, Frederick, and Nick. Millie asked, "So, are you reborn Goth or modern Emo?"

E.V. placed the last bite of sandwich into her mouth, refrained from responding while she chewed, and replied, "I don't subscribe to labels." She stood up, nodded to the group, and walked to the trash can where she promptly delivered the wrappers from her home lunch.

Later that afternoon, the hallways were busy with students at their lockers before the last period of the day. E.V. felt a presence and eyes upon her. She looked up before hearing his voice. "Hey, I'm Nick D'Angelino." She recognized him from the group who had stopped at her table during the lunch period.

"E.V.," she reported flatly.

"Cool," he responded. "Maybe we can hang out some time."

"Maybe," she nodded with a grin that left her mouth so quickly it could have been missed.

Nick continued to meet E.V. at the end of each school day. She thought he seemed nice enough. They shared no classes, but he began to tuck small notes and sketches into E.V.'s locker. The pictures were interesting to her. They were mostly animals, guitars, and cars. Well, she pondered, I like animals, music, and do hope for a car someday. E.V. appreciated Nick's drawing talents. She, herself, loved to create art.

One Friday afternoon, she opened her locker and saw a small envelope. E.V. quickly looked to her left and then to her right. No one was at either adjacent locker. With a hint of excitement and cautious optimism, she unsealed the mystery. It was an unfinished pencil sketch of two people dancing. She replaced the paper into the envelope, tucked it inside her bag, and turned around.

"Well?" Nick smiled.

"Well?" E.V. repeated with a curious playfulness while she tried not to overreact with surprise.

The young man took a breath. "Would you like to go with me to the dance next Friday?"

Her response was quick. "I'll have to check."

"Whether anyone else asks you?" he pumped.

She replied carefully, "No, I'll have to check with my grandmother. We, uh, kind of take care of one another." E.V. shrugged, "I really don't dance."

His answer was neutral. "That's cool. Would you let me know by Monday, E.V., and can I have your phone number?"

"I'll give you an answer to both questions after the weekend." The two nodded in agreement. They turned and walked in opposite directions.

On her way home, E.V. tried not to make a big deal about it in her own mind. She was plainly pleased, but there were questions. Why did Nick only approach at her locker? He seemed interested. However, they had only briefly met once in the cafeteria when he was with others friends. Hmm, she wondered. Maybe he's shy. She could be fine with that reasoning. Then again, she classified his random pop-up appearances as a bit creepy.

E.V. had a few other acquaintances she would talk with during school or message when off campus. However, she didn't feel comfortable sharing thoughts, opinions, or questions regarding Nick with anyone her own age. On their way home after church that Sunday, E.V. drove with Ruby. She had obtained her learner's permit and was able to drive with Florida state-enforced learner's restrictions.

"Grams?"

"Mm-hmm?"

"A boy from school asked me to the dance at the end of the week."

"E.V., please pull in at the shopping center on the right," the woman pointed.

The girl didn't question the request. She turned the car inside a parking space and asked whether her grandmother needed something from the store. "I'm happy to run in and get whatever you need, Grams."

The woman stared at her granddaughter. "You're so talented and beautiful, Eves. I figured you'd have a boyfriend sooner or later."

"Grams, he's not my boyfriend. I barely know him. That's why I'm running this by you. You're the only one I trust," she stated plainly.

Ruby looked down and dabbed at the corner of her eye with a tissue and again looked up. "Evangeline, I can still imagine you as that precious little baby who came home with G-pa Bill and me." After a short pause, "Well, how do you feel about that boy and the dance?"

"We don't have any classes together, so I can't say I know him well. Some kids recently approached me in the cafeteria. He was one of them. A few of us were dressed similarly and they struck up a brief conversation. I rarely see that group at lunch. They must leave campus."

"Okay, Evangeline, but what about the boy?"

"He draws, leaves me little notes, and seems nice."

"Do you want to go to the dance, E.V.?"

"Yeah, kind of," she hesitated.

Ruby gently concluded, "Trust your gut, girl. If you don't feel comfortable going alone with him, meet him there. Maybe you can go with some of your girlfriends."

E.V. smiled at the term, girlfriends, but she understood that her grandmother was from another generation. "Good idea, Grams. Thanks."

That night, E.V. sent a group message to Scarlett, Emma, and Destiny. After she had hit the ball against Grams, her best sounding board, she was able to bounce it off her friends. All three girls agreed to meet and take E.V. with them to the dance. Emma was the eldest and had been driving since the summer. They seemed happy enough that E.V. had a date, even though none of them did. Emma offered that Nick seemed pretty laid-back in the co-ed P.E. class they were both in. Destiny messaged that she was happy for E.V., and Scarlett typed a dot to indicate she was following the story.

Monday morning arrived with, as Grandpa Bill was known to say, break neck speed. However, the day dragged. When E.V. arrived at her locker at the end of the day, Nick was already waiting for her. He looked nervous.

"Hi," E.V. began, "and yes," she smiled for a bit longer than usual.

"Wha-what?" he stammered and took a side step away from the girl's locker.

"Yes, I'd like to meet you at the dance."

The boy hesitated. "Meet me?" He paused. "Oh, oh, I get it. Of course, that would be fine and—safe."

"Well, just in case things don't quite work out," E.V. softened her typical forward demeanor.

"Sure, and that takes the pressure off both of us. You're pretty smart," he laughed, "and pretty."

E.V. smiled. "Well, I guess I'll see you at the dance or maybe before Friday at my locker." They both giggled and said goodbye.

The rest of the week was a series of notes, drawings, and paper flowers pushed through the doors and slats of E.V.'s locker. One day, Nick even bought a school lunch and sat next to E.V. in the cafeteria without his other friends. He offered her his brownie. She thanked him but declined. She found it amusing that out of the group of his friends who approached her on the day they met, Nick was the one who was dressed least like her. He was more of a tee-shirt, jeans, and boots kind of a guy with a black baseball cap and hair longer than E.V.'s.

When she had shared that detail with her friends, in a four-way group message that evening, it was Destiny who had branded E.V. as smitten. E.V. didn't respond, but Emma added that Nick was cute. Scarlett sent a thumbs-up image. E.V. shook her head and smiled. Maybe they were right, she wondered. She refused to commit one way or the other.

Ruby noticed that her granddaughter was spending more time getting ready for school every morning. She's growing up, Ruby mused in silence. After dinner, two nights before the dance, Ruby asked E.V. whether she needed a new dress or outfit for the event.

"No thanks," was the teen's only response while she finished washing the dishes. E.V. then pulled an apple from the fridge, rinsed it at the kitchen sink, and stated that she was going to her room to study. Ruby nodded and stared into a flashback of Bonnie getting ready for a school dance. How that girl loved new clothes, Ruby recollected. She couldn't bring to mind Bonnie's first or last dance before the dearly departed daughter graduated from high school. Ruby let out a small sigh. Bonnie was out of the house on most nights during her teen years. A pang of guilt pulled at and twisted Ruby's intestines. Shame for parental leniency bore into the woman's spirit.

Chapter Four

A NEW DOOR

Since Bill had passed away, Ruby acknowledged that she thought even more about Bonnie, their only daughter. To Ruby, it felt like memories were strung together without a distinct beginning or end. Specific associations melded with vague recollections. The aging woman, once sharp enough to be chosen as a potential astronaut, strained her mental faculties and associated pathways in order to separate which instances were about young Bonnie, Bradley, or E.V. Bonnie was often present in Ruby's memory and was at times, interchanged for E.V. Ruby decided to bring it up at her next appointment with Dr. Davis.

"Look, Doc, I just can't see why mixed-up memories about my family could be connected to Challenger."

"Ruby," the woman began, "the shuttle disaster was a traumatic event for the whole country as well as for people in many other parts of the world. You were so close to it. Dreams, friends, and visions died on that day. You had also lost your daughter when she was young and adopted her baby as your own. According to you, your son had his own issues, and Bill, your best friend and support, has died. Evangeline, in many ways, has taken the place of all that you miss. From what you've shared, Ruby, Evangeline is her own person and could be described as a strong teen. I would very much like to meet her in person.

"Well, that would be something," Ruby shook her head, looked down for a moment, and chuckled.

The psychologist continued, "You've insisted that you want that shuttle door tightly sealed behind you, Ruby. Yet it needs to be fully opened and dealt with, so we can first clean out everything associated with it and then, shut it gently behind you instead of slamming it and walking away. The contents of stuffed closets always have a way of tumbling down on us when we open the door to retrieve something, even when we try to block the items from falling off shelves. We also need to explore the positives that resulted from your connections with the space program."

Ruby waited. She stared at the therapist and then took a deep, shaky breath. "Years ago, I was getting closer to being the runner-up for the citizen-astronaut to join the Challenger Space Shuttle mission team." She paused. "There had been thousands of applicants. The numbers were whittled down to just a handful of us. During one of the training sessions, I was sent to a specialist after complaining of a piercing headache and then diagnosed with a retinal detachment. Because of the imminent eye surgery and recovery time, I never re-entered the program. On January 28, 1986, the space shuttle lifted into its final ascent, and barely more than one minute later, suffered a catastrophic explosion, propelling all on board into eternity. That's all," Ruby stated.

"Ruby, you shared more with me before. There was guilt, the unexpected death of your father shortly thereafter, and I believe you also referred to a reconciliation."

The elderly lady shifted uncomfortably in her chair and used the cane to reposition herself, "Yes, reconciliation meant I made peace."

"Do you feel that peace?" the professional asked.

After another lengthy pause, "No."

The long silence prompted the doctor. "What else, Ruby? Let's clean out that closet filled with your very real trauma and pain."

"I sensed in my heart," Ruby began with stilted movement of her speech, "that the Good Lord still had work for me to accomplish on Earth. I guess he preserved my fate from an early demise. However, I was never fully able to squelch the guilt about not being on that craft." She began to speak more naturally, "I also experienced overwhelming sadness caused by the sudden and tragic death of my own father within that same period of time."

The doctor began slowly but directly, "As you focused on other life experiences, your memories, outside of your conscious awareness, became distorted. Our brains try to protect us. Think of it like a cushion from trauma."

Ruby wrinkled her brow, "Really? How?" She understood the words but was perplexed by the deeper meaning and its application.

The psychologist stood up from her desk and moved over to a dry erase board mounted on an adjacent wall. She lifted and uncapped a marker that had been resting on the metal ledge. The doctor began to draw a vertical column of rectangles. Inside each rectangle, Dr. Davis wrote a word or phrase that identified a distinct event that caused what she referred to as knots for Ruby. Examples were the space shuttle, Bonnie's death, and Bill's death. Adjacent to that column, Dr. Davis created an array of ovals on the smooth white surface. Within each empty oval shell, the doctor jotted down separate emotional perceptions that Ruby identified as joy, excitement, pleasure, satisfaction, grief, loneliness, anxiety, and despair. In a third column of circles, Ruby was to list her achievements. Next, the doctor asked Ruby to identify where there were connections. As Ruby pointed out one, then two, and more, the doctor chose separately colored markers to draw arrows from one shape to another. In some cases, lines were drawn with arrows pointing to and intersecting multiple rectangles, ovals, and circles.

"Ruby, over the years, you spent much time justifying your reasons and feelings instead of getting help. Thankfully, you're motivated to receive treatment now. As you are well aware, that's where the work is. Kudos to you for being willing to roll up your sleeves, and get it done."

Ruby responded with clarity, "I can now see the connections, Doctor. I want to be the best person I can be for E.V., so she can live as normal a life as possible."

"Like I've said, we should all meet together as well as individually." While Dr. Davis spoke, she referred back to the diagram and pointed with a marker. She moved back to her desk and sat down. "You've also experienced guilt for your depression." The psychologist glanced down at her notes and then back up toward Ruby. "Your two children, Bradley and Bonnie, were both under the age of ten when they thought their mom would be a famous astronaut. And then, they moved forward toward adulthood. You mentioned more than once that Bill often tried to make light of the situation to protect you. No family member, probably not even your husband, benefitted from that. You shared that Bill suggested the family move to a different state after the Challenger incident, but you remained in a rural and remote part of Florida where you were still able to feel a connection to the space program."

"All truth, Doc, but I can't figure how every part fits together."

"Please keep journal notes about the pieces, Ruby. You can even draw diagrams like we just did together on the dry erase board. Then, bring the journal to our next session."

Ruby made another appointment at the front desk before making her way to the parking lot. She thought about E.V. going to the dance that evening with her friends. Ruby said a silent prayer that God would keep her granddaughter and all the adolescents safe, which immediately connected the dots that made the woman think about how dissimilar Bonnie and Bradley were from E.V. Ruby got home in time to see E.V. before her friends picked her up. How kids dress for a dance these days, the grandmother silently thought and shook her head. The two shared a quick hug goodbye, and E.V. was in the car as the girls backed out of the driveway.

Ruby remembered a time when Bradley was excited to go to a high school dance. He came home with a blackened eye and rumpled clothing. When Bill said he would talk to the other boy, Bradley simply answered, "I deserved it." After that, there were girlfriends and dates but no further mention of dances. That was a rectangle for Brad, and he must have connected his own ovals, Ruby mused. She secretly hoped it had not been a circle for her rebellious boy.

Ruby permitted herself to be pierced by another memory as if the mental pleasure of seeing her daughter would strip away its associated punishing agonies. Bonnie and Ted were young when they learned about the pregnancy. His parents offered to pay for an abortion. A year later, Bonnie confided in her mother that early on the day of the scheduled termination, she had called her best friend, Paula. Bonnie whispered a dream to Paula that she had carried her baby to full term and then gave birth to a most precious infant. Bonnie recounted to her friend that when she peered into the large blue-gray eyes of the child, she felt a bond. The baby was a girl and beautiful. In the dream, Bonnie held the newborn and knew that she was special. A story unfurled. She never saw Ted again and kept her own last name for the child, Evangeline Gold.

A few hours had passed, and E.V. assessed that she was having a decent time at the dance. There wasn't much dancing, but she and Nick relaxed enough to talk and get to know one another better. E.V.'s three friends, who she arrived with, kept going into the bathroom together. So, when Nick asked if he could drive his date home, she answered, "Sure, why not?"

After Scarlett, Emma, and Destiny emerged from the restroom once again, E.V. whispered that she was leaving with Nick. She then ducked inside the lavatory to text her grandmother that the young man would be taking her home. "Do you feel safe, Eves?" Ruby typed. Before responding, E.V. looked up and spotted the trio of toadstools from her past. They had been busy fixing their hair and makeup at the mirrors. The girls avoided eye contact with E.V., and all three brushed past her toward the exit as a giant, collective tumbleweed with eye rolls, short exhales, and one brave snicker.

"I do, Grams." E.V. touched the send button.

"Make sure you keep your tracker device on," Grams typed.

The girl smiled, "Location sharing is on, Grams." Then E.V. added, "And you, too! I want to know where my Grams is at all times!" She knew that would make her grandmother chuckle. When E.V. started driving, Ruby shared her anxiety with Dr. Davis, who recommended that she and Evangeline both add the locator app to their cell phones.

E.V. knew it would be fine to ride home with Nick but silently reminded herself that the inner knowings, as she liked to call the phenomena, were not always as accurate for herself. The evening had been fun so far, yet she suddenly allowed herself to indulge in a few flashbacks. E.V. recalled that when just a child, she knew that her mother would not be there for her. She knew that she'd never get to meet her father. E.V. knew that her grandmother would ultimately need her more than she needed the aging woman. She also knew details about some of her school acquaintances. There was that one Friday night, E.V. remembered, when she dreamed that a teacher was in a rollover accident. The following Monday, additional counselors were brought in for the students before an announcement was made about the fatal wreck.

She was called crazy, strange, a witch; students said her name, E.V., was short for evil. They also made fun that she was the twin of Eve from the garden of Eden who encountered the snake and brought evil upon women and men. However, Evangeline had to admit to herself that oftentimes, she did know things that were beyond reason.

Nevertheless, E.V. always felt that some piece was missing. She never knew the origins of those sensations about events and was typically only aware when something bad was about to happen. Her grandmother often called them omens. She discouraged E.V. from announcing them, especially to the pastor or congregants of their tiny church assembly where Ruby, Bill, and E.V. had faithfully attended for years. As E.V. matured, she mentioned her inklings less and less. E.V. shook off the memories and met Nick back near the dance floor.

He held a hand out to E.V. with a boyish look on his face, "We should dance at least once, tonight."

She nodded and was relieved that it wasn't a slow dance. E.V. judged it as the darkest song of the evening, but it had somehow been approved by the assistant principal. When the song ended, the two ate some snacks, drank punch, and finally headed to Nick's car. They talked, laughed, and were soon at E.V.'s house. He walked his date to the door, gave her a quick hug, and thanked E.V. for a great time.

"Yeah, you too, Nick." He was backing his car out of the driveway before she even had a chance to process what had just happened or did not happen. After all, E.V. had wondered how the date might end. It had been like hanging out with any of her other friends, but then again, it was different. She stepped inside.

Ruby joined her granddaughter in the kitchen, "Hey, Eves, how was the dance?"

The teen opened an upper kitchen cabinet and removed a glass before she retrieved a container of milk from the fridge. She poured herself a cup and replaced the milk. "It was fine, Grams." She shut the refrigerator door.

"Did you have fun?"

E.V. took a sip and thought for a moment. "I actually did."

At the end of school on Monday, Nick was promptly at E.V.'s locker. The two exchanged greetings. Nick asked if he could have E.V.'s phone number. She acquiesced. He pulled out his phone, added her as a contact, and then sent her a message so she had his number.

"I really had a good time last Friday," he quietly offered.

Her response was smooth, "Yeah, me too."

Nick offered, "May I drive you home from school? It's on my way to work."

"No, thanks," and then she added, "not this time."

"Okay," he uttered, "then I'll walk you to your bus."

"Sounds good," E.V. decided aloud.

The two made their way to the line of parked school buses. As they approached, Nick cleared his throat and asked, "Would it be all right if I borrow the drawing that I put into your locker to ask you to the dance?"

"Let me see if it's still in my backpack," E.V. responded with hesitation while she wondered about the motive behind his question. She opened the pack and drew out the envelope. The puzzled girl handed it to Nick with a nod, "Here you go."

"Thanks, E.V.," he replied with a grin. "Talk to you, soon."

During the bus ride home, E.V. wondered if that's how couples broke up. She had no idea, never having been part of a couple before. According to E.V.'s own analysis, she had already put too much time into the question and perhaps into Nick. After all, she tried to convince herself, it was just a meaningless high school dance. She needed to get home, do chores, take care of her rabbit and chickens, housed in the backyard, and then do homework if and only if there was any time left.

Since Driver's Ed. class had ended, new evening electives were being offered by the school. E.V. enjoyed getting out two nights per week, so she signed up for an art elective apart from the mainstream coursework offered during the day. As more of her friends became licensed drivers, Ruby no longer needed to take E.V. or pick her up on most nights. E.V. worked at a horse farm on the weekends, where she cleaned stalls and water tubs, so her weeknights remained open.

On the first night of class, E.V. was drawn to the school's art room. The smells of paint, paper, markers, clay, cardboard, and freshly-sharpened pencils permeated the space and captivated Evangeline Gold. She moved about the easels that displayed many works of varying degrees of artistic abilities, talents, and techniques.

After the instructor asked the group to be seated, she began to take attendance. One lone student hurried into the room. It was Nick. "Sorry," he announced, "I just got out of work." The teacher nodded and waited for him to find a place at a table with an empty chair, which happened to be right next to E.V. She looked down because she felt the boy's discomfort. The teacher started to explain the house-keeping rules of the course.

E.V. had experienced no lunch date or locker visit that day at school. Part of her felt renewed. Part of her remained cautious, while the rest of E.V. was still annoyed that Nick requested the dance invitation be returned to him.

The students were each asked to write what they knew about art and what they wanted to learn. As everyone began to record their ideas, Nick glanced at E.V. and whispered, "Hi."

"Hey," she whispered back.

They had broken the ice and seemed to take up exactly where they left off. During a ten-minute break at the halfway point in the class, E.V. stepped out of the room to stretch her legs. She thought about passing by the Christian youth group meeting but it was on the second floor of the opposite end of the high school. She turned, and there he was, Nick, bounding behind her like an oversized puppy dog. She had to laugh.

"Hey, E.V.," he panted slightly as he strode alongside her. "I wasn't in school today and missed seeing you. My mom needed help with the twins. They're much younger than me, you know, different dad and all. Anyway, nice surprise seeing you in this class."

"Why'd you ask for the dance invitation back?" E.V. was not one to mince words.

"Just borrowing it," he smiled.

"I see; I think," E.V. returned a quick smile.

By the end of the second week of art club, E.V. was getting rides to night school with friends, and Nick was driving her home after every class. She was starting to feel comfortable with the young man. They mostly talked and got to know one another better. Grams would always be awake, reading and sipping hot tea at the kitchen table when E.V. got home. After the third night, Grams had a plate of oatmeal cookies on the table. She patted E.V.'s chair, and the girl took a seat.

"Well?" the woman began.

E.V.'s response was casual, "The class is fine. I'm learning new shading techniques."

Ruby nodded once and moved her open hand with fingers together toward herself as if she beckoned the girl to come closer. E.V. understood that her grandmother was her guardian in so many ways. It was obvious to the young woman that Ruby wanted more details. With a soft smile and quiet voice, E.V. continued, "Grams, Nick is sweet and kind. He is very talented and intelligent, too. It's okay, Grams."

"It's important to be surrounded by folks who have a healthy fear of the Lord. Does he know Jesus?" E.V. shrugged in silence. Ruby continued, "Does he treat you with respect, Eves?"

Evangeline was reminded of the prayer she had overheard on break during the first night of Driver's Ed. about being an example of Christ and being surrounded by others who aspired to do the same. There was a pause before she answered, "I believe so, Grams."

Chapter Five

LAY THEM STRAIGHT

Nick invited E.V. to join him during the high school festival and fundraiser. E.V. had previously mentioned her interest in attending. Their art club sponsored an arcade game booth to raise money for supplies. The class had designated three evenings to build and paint the stand. Students alternated between working on the booth while others moved through centers to practice a variety of art techniques they were learning about. Like the dance, it was held on a Friday evening after school. Nick and E.V. decided to sign up for the same shift so they could also enjoy the festivities when they weren't volunteering.

Younger students from the elementary and middle schools, as well as local folks, were all invited to attend. E.V. and Nick's art class stayed after school that Friday afternoon to set up their area. The instructor treated her students to pizza. Food created a captive work audience.

Before the gates opened, E.V. excused herself from her class-mates. She instantly noticed that the Christian ministry club had a booth with a small stage attached. The students were setting up, tuning their instruments, and organizing what looked like colorful bookmarks at their booth's counter. A girl and boy were laughing as they stapled student-created posters to the framed housing made of wood. E.V. was drawn to the table and began to silently read the sayings and Bible verses on the neatly trimmed cardstock.

"They're called tracts. Hi, I'm Pete," he smiled. "Go ahead, help yourself."

She picked up what still appeared to be a bookmark, looked at it, and tucked it into the back pocket of her jeans. E.V. looked up and immediately recognized the young man with the guitar strapped over his shoulder. "Oh, hi," she began. "You're from the school club, right? I'm E.V." She lifted her palm to give a short wave, but Pete had already extended his for a warm handshake.

"Hello, E.V." He released her hand. "Is that short for another name?"

"Evangeline."

He nodded. His hair had grown out since the last time she saw him during evening school clubs, and his curly bangs bobbed up and down. "I really like your name, Evangeline."

"Thanks, but I had nothing to do with it," she shrugged. "Guess it was my mother's choice," she retorted.

"That's funny!" he reacted.

Nick jogged up to meet them, "Hey, hey, E.V.!"

She found the volume of his voice to be rather loud and his tone a bit squeaky. "Nick, this is Pete. He's from the Christian Ministry Club." The two boys nodded. Before Pete offered his hand, Nick interrupted, "E.V., we have to get back."

"Okay, see you, Pete," she stated. That time, Pete gave a brief wave as the couple turned to walk back to their booth. E.V. shrugged off Nick's behavior, but tucked it inside her mental notes.

People had begun to arrive. One of the games at the art club booth was a jump rope contest held every fifteen minutes. Most of the contenders were elementary school-aged children, who lined up to turn in their tickets for a chance to win a prize. After the first hour, E.V. continued to check the time. Listening to the same nursery rhymes over and over again, as kids jumped rope, made E.V. want to pull her hair out. Between alphabet songs, name songs, and the one that drove her most crazy, which began with one-two, buckle and something about a shoe, she was taking deep breaths to help her plow through to the end of the shift. Just as two girls approached to relieve E.V. and Nick, he shouted with a laugh, "Hey, wait, my mom and sisters are here and want to play!"

E.V. was quick to reply, "You go right ahead. I'll look around the fair. Come find me if you want, Nick."

After brief introductions between E.V. and his family, Nick turned away. E.V. began to walk toward the other booths. Pick-up sticks and giant, hefty hens still tormented her ears and mind. Suddenly, Destiny called out, "Hey, girl!"

E.V. turned, and the two greeted one another. Destiny told her that Emma and Scarlett were busy working a booth for their business elective class, so E.V. and Destiny decided to hang out. E.V. took note that Frederick and Callista also worked the business booth. The two girls each bought a bag of popcorn from their friends' Projected Marketing Teams Club. E.V. suggested that they work their way over to check out the music coming from the Christian Ministry booth. Some students were dancing to the rhythms while others were picking up tracts and speaking to the man who led the classes each week. E.V. recognized his voice.

A different rhythm broke through just as the sun started to set. Destiny tapped E.V.'s arm. Two of the three toadstools, as E.V. liked to call them, were holding hands and dancing. One wore a men's-style suit jacket. Other people soon joined them. By E.V.'s estimation, some were definitely too old to be high school students but neither did they match what E.V. deemed to be a slice of the "parental cross section." It seemed awkward and out of place to her. They sported rainbow shirts and caps with slogans.

Suddenly, objects flew. Then, one of the ministry students who had been playing bass guitar and a second guy on the drums, both abruptly jumped off the stage. One shouted, "Oh, no you don't! None of you should be here! This is Christian music! You're despicable!"

Then, Nick's friends, who had met E.V. in the cafeteria weeks before, came to the female couple's defense. The one guy with glasses, named Frederick, tried to calm everyone down. The girl who had first spoken to E.V. about her clothes shouted above the chaos, "Where's Nick?"

"Millie, right?" E.V. questioned but didn't wait for the girl to respond. She simply nodded toward the booth around the corner. Teenagers were being slammed against the Christian Club wooden structure in an absurd scene. Tracts flew up and into the air and were then trampled and ground into the dirt. E.V. was busy trying to separate those on opposing sides. She let a few curse words fly from her lips.

E.V. could still hear part of the song droning from where she left Nick, "Seven, eight, lay them straight ..." E.V. thought it was a nightmare. This just wasn't happening at her school. When the pushing began, she tried to back away. Soon, cops arrived and were pulling people apart in the crowd. E.V. was roughly handled and pushed down onto a grassy area.

Pete, ushered by two policemen, was urged onto the ground next to E.V. "You all right, Evangeline?" Pete checked.

"Cool party," she rolled her eyes and exhaled.

The setting was surreal. Some people never knew that the ruckus had taken place. Others were directly involved. Bystanders were also pulled in. Those accused of harming others were arrested. The remaining students involved were led to the gym, questioned, and released to their parents and guardians.

Pete's father had to speak with police, parents, and the school principal. He finally came over to where Pete was seated on the floor. "Let's go, Son. We're done, here."

Pete spoke quietly, "Please, Dad, I'd prefer to stay with Evangeline a little longer. She's waiting for her grandmother."

The man looked at his son and then nodded toward E.V., "I'm Pastor Dave."

"Evangeline," she noted as they shook hands.

She felt a lump lodge in her throat when Ruby walked through the double doors of the gym. Grams had to sign E.V. out and pick her up as if E.V. had gone against school rules or the law. The woman looked worried, angry, old. She and E.V. met. There were brief introductions with Pastor Dave and his son before the two families parted ways.

On the way home, Grams and E.V. were both quiet. Once seated at the kitchen table, Ruby spoke first as she waited for the water to boil in the tea kettle. "When I got the notification, Eves, it took me right back to the horrendous calls I used to field from the police about your mom and uncle. It sounded like you were just in the wrong place at the wrong time. Is that true?"

"Yes, Grams. It was just awful. People were pushing and screaming and worst of all, disrespecting one another. Don't get me wrong, some of those on the attack and being attacked were jerks! But so-called Christians were judgmental of two girls who started dancing together before other similar couples joined in. I wasn't even sure where the others came from. Grams, it was all preplanned. I just know it. The girls, and then others who joined in the dancing, wore obvious paraphernalia. They were looking for attention and wanted to get things riled up. I'm sure I saw the media there."

Ruby exclaimed, "Of all the cockamamie, cultural, and emotional setups!"

"So, do you also think it could have been staged, Grams?"

Ruby nodded. She had already decided; her granddaughter was innocent that time. "Where was Nick?"

"Good question, Grams. I don't know the answer. He was actually acting weird the whole afternoon."

"Who was that boy with the curly hair standing with you in the gym?" enquired Ruby.

"Oh, that was Pete. He's part of the Christian Ministry Club. I just found out tonight that his dad is the pastor or maybe, the youth pastor. They seem pretty cool."

"The pastor's son is cute, Eves," Ruby nodded.

"Grams!" E.V. giggled. "I'm glad he wasn't one who attacked others. Pete also told his dad that he wanted to wait for you to come get me. It was," E.V. paused, "very sweet."

Ruby remained silent as she poured a cup of tea. "Evangeline, you do realize the sort of immoral behavior suggested by that particular dancing is frowned upon in both the Old and New Testaments, right?"

"The Bible says not to judge," was E.V.'s comeback.

"Well, E.V., you already determined that some of the young people were jerks." Both women in the kitchen were obviously drained and had grown short-tempered.

"Night, Grams. I love you."

The woman placed her tea cup on the table, "Love you, too." They shared their customary hug. Ruby never hugged Bonnie good-night on that last one. She vowed to never miss another.

E.V. went into the bathroom to brush her teeth and begin the cleansing routine to remove her makeup before bed. A wave of exhaustion washed over her. E.V. stared at herself in the mirror and wondered in silence whether she even looked like Bonnie. She only had a few pictures to compare herself and Bonnie as teens. E.V. got into bed and noticed that Nick had messaged her. He only reported being sorry that he had to leave so soon. E.V. shook her head as she pulled up the lightweight blanket. She concluded no response was needed.

E.V. stayed awake for what felt like a long time, even though she was fatigued. Her mind replayed the events from that afternoon and evening. She knew what she knew but wasn't able to make sense of the rest of it. She got up for a drink of water and hoped that her mind would slow down enough to drift off to sleep when she went back to bed. She had to wake up early for her Saturday job with the horses. E.V. affirmed to herself with a sigh that she mostly preferred working with animals over people.

She lay there and stared at the moonlight that reflected through an opening in the blinds. It materialized onto part of the ceiling and spilled down the wall as if it originated from a movie theater projection lamp, which brought to mind the few memories that remained of her mother. They were always in the same order of her mental slideshow. The first was at the beach. Teenage Bonnie, clad in a floral bikini, was playing volleyball with a group of friends. E.V. assumed the image was set in her mind from the picture she kept in her collection.

The second remembrance was a joy-filled occasion for E.V. It was her second birthday. She ate cake and then proudly strutted around the house with a new doll and toy stroller. Bonnie was there, giggling, as she attempted to create a name for the toy baby. Then, a much younger Grams popped her head into the room and suggested the name, Mary. E.V. was later reminded that the name, Mary, stuck. However, E.V. could only pronounce it as Mimi. After that, the whole family always called the baby doll, Mimi. The doll remained on a shelf in E.V.'s bedroom closet.

Once in a while, Grams still brought up E.V.'s imaginary childhood friends. One was named Mimi by young Evangeline. Her grandparents understood where that name originated. When E.V. turned four, she told everyone that Mimi was lonely, so Sam came to play. As a child, E.V. often asked whether she had brothers or sisters and if so, where they were. She would frequently tell her grandparents that Sam was coming with them to the store, on errands, or even to the old white-washed church building shared by a few denominations that scheduled their services throughout the weekend at different times. Bill would just laugh and shake his head, while Ruby would nod. Ruby assured her husband that it was normal for an only child to have imaginary friends.

The final set of memories were all connected to being left alone in the crib and crying for long periods of time. Ultimately, Grams would go into the room and sing E.V. back to sleep, or it would be

G-pa Bill, always ready with a cup of water and a story to be told. The tale was usually about an adventurous young bear who would climb into G-pa Bear's lap and fall asleep. Frequently, the grandfather also slipped into slumber while telling the story, then got up an hour later, and tried to quietly leave without waking the child. Bonnie was usually out of the house or too high or drunk to respond.

Chapter Six

WAVES

The next morning arrived far too quickly for E.V. She dressed, grabbed a quick breakfast, and made her lunch. Grams drove E.V. and dropped her off at the horse farm. It was a quiet ride. At lunchtime, Nick messaged E.V. to ask if he could take her to dinner to make up for his quick departure the night before. E.V. hesitated but then, said yes. He offered to pick her up straight from work. She objected that she would need to clean up after working around horses all day.

He insisted that they needed to talk, so instead of going out, he would bring a picnic dinner they could share at the beach. Okay, she thought and looked down at her dusty clothes and mud-washed boots. Nick obviously does not spend time with horses, she concluded. E.V. called her grandmother before the end of her lunch break. Grams wanted to know which beach and what time they'd be home. E.V. promised to get her the information.

Nick arrived on time. He gave E.V. a hug. She offered him a short tour of the farm and barn. He nodded in agreement but seemed far away. He didn't ask any questions about the place or E.V.'s love for and knowledge about horses. They walked to his car. She opened the passenger-side door at the same time Nick sat down in the driver's seat. As E.V. snugged into the bucket seat of his old sports car, she caught him staring. She raised her eyebrows, "What?"

"Uh, you look nice," he smiled.

"Thanks."

"I've never seen you wear a ponytail or baseball cap," he offered.

She smirked, "I wouldn't have my hair professionally done to muck stalls and scrub water troughs."

"Guess not," he smiled. "Anyway, my mom was hosting a group at the house, so I hope you like sandwiches and sides. She told me to help myself."

"Sure," E.V. stated. She was trying to figure out what was so different about Nick.

He grew pensive and then, "E.V., I'm sorry for leaving in such a hurry the other night."

"Why?" she immediately retorted,

Nick stared at the road. "Well, we came together, so I should have taken you home. Then, when things got kind out of hand, my mom was worried about my little sisters."

"Sure, I could see that happening—"

"—It's just that you seem to be able to take care of yourself," in haste, he cut her off. E.V. was silent. Oh, I can definitely take care of myself, she silently maintained. Nick turned up the music and added, "This weather is what my family refers to as Florida balmy, but with the sun scheduled to set in under an hour, it should cool off. Plus, it's always breezy at the beach."

Small talk about the weather was the only conversation that transpired during the rest of the ride. E.V. wished she had turned Nick down for the date. Yet, her knower knew this was supposed to happen for a bigger reason. The car pulled in at a sandy parking area of a raw beach that E.V. had never been to before.

"This is it," Nick announced.

He got out of the car and popped the trunk. E.V. grabbed the blanket, and Nick took the cooler. The rhythmic sound of the waves automatically lulled E.V.'s emotions back to happy times with her grandparents.

As they neared the water, a woman jogged along its edge. A man and three children were laughing as they repeatedly threw sticks into the water, and two dogs continued to fetch them. One dog never seemed quite sure whether it really wanted to relinquish the twig to any human. A game of tug-of-war took place every time until the pet once again, chased the lure.

"How's this?" Nick asked.

E.V. quickly eyed the open area that was blocked off on one side by knotted driftwood, sporadically wrapped with dried seaweed. Bits of old garbage were also locked onto and around the base of the rough, natural art display. "Looks okay," she surmised aloud. E.V. attempted to lighten the mood. "Maybe we can bring the driftwood montage back to our art club for extra points."

"We're gonna need all the points we can get," sighed Nick as he and E.V. set out the beach blanket on top of the sand. "Hey, what happened was crazy. I bet all the admin are sitting around this weekend, wondering how to apply group punishment and call it justice."

E.V.'s response was a little too quick, "No, no, they're worrying about getting sued."

Nick had just seated himself on the ground cover and his head whipped to one side and faced E.V. "Why would you say that?"

She shrugged, "Just a guess," she cringed inside. E.V. did not want to share such a vivid, illustrated knowing.

Nick's furrowed brow softened when he opened the cooler and brought out some of the food. "Please, E.V., help yourself." She took note of the colorful cans mixed in alongside water bottles. E.V.'s questioning expression was enough to make Nick laugh, "They're RTDs."

She started, "RDs ..."

He spoke more slowly, "RTDs, you know, Ready to Drink; they're like cocktails. Go ahead, and pick a flavor. Enjoy." He took one for himself.

"Thanks, Nick." She retrieved a wrapped sandwich and a bottle of water.

"That's cool, E.V."

They shared a bag of chips and ate the sandwiches and then put the rest of the food back into the ice chest. Once again, Nick motioned toward the alcoholic beverages as he helped himself to another container. E.V. put up one hand, "No, thanks."

They sat, watching the sunlight dim as the swells approached and lapped upon the shore. Nick pulled himself closer to her. His arm was around E.V. He kissed her gently at first but then pressed in. She pushed him away. "I don't think so, Nick."

"But, E.V., you're so beautiful," he breathed.

"But I said, no," E.V. persisted. Intrusive yet liberating headlights illuminated the area just as she moved farther away from Nick and stood up.

"Hey! We have company!" Nick seemed unaffected by her refusal and elated about the additions. Some cars pulled in, and a number of teens joined Nick and E.V. They brought beer, sodas, and more chips. A bonfire was built, and Nick continued to drink while night fell.

E.V. was intrigued by the experience. She found it interesting that none of Nick's acquaintances, except for Millie, were the ones he hung out with at school. E.V. checked her cell phone. It was after 10 p.m. She leaned over and told Nick that she needed to be home by her curfew.

He kissed her again. "Just relax, E.V. Here, try some of this." Nick reached over to another guy who passed him a joint. He held the weird-looking cigarette up to E.V.'s face.

She instantly recoiled. "Not happening, dude," emphasized E.V. Nick took a hit and sent the drug back. "Look," E.V. declared, "if you want to stay here with your playmates, I'll find a ride home."

Millie was listening. "Come on, Nick, time to go, buddy." She turned and whispered something to the boy who she had ridden with.

It was decided. E.V. would drive Nick's car, and Millie and Tom would follow them to E.V.'s house. Then, Tom would drive Nick home, and Millie would follow. Nick was in no shape to get behind the wheel. While E.V. waited for them to help her date load up his belongings, she messaged Grams that she'd be home in under an hour. E.V. also promised Grams that her location would show up on the grandmother's cell phone. E.V. wondered in silence whether Nick's mother truly and knowingly provided the alcohol. She was thankful that he slept most of the way to her house.

E.V. sighed with relief when she stepped into her own kitchen. The lights were dim, so she figured that Ruby had gone to bed. She heard her grandmother in the hallway before the woman entered the kitchen. "You okay, Eves?"

"Sure, Grams. Why?"

Ruby flipped on brighter lights and studied her granddaughter's face. "Want to tell me about it, child?" Ruby sat down at the kitchen table. E.V. joined her grandmother, who knew her so well.

E.V. didn't hesitate, "I'm pretty sure I'll break it off with Nick. He was weirder than ever, and he was all over me."

"Well, Eves, I support your decision. That's how some boys can be."

"Immature boys," E.V. added. "Nick also brought alcohol. He didn't pressure me, and I didn't partake." Ruby listened. "Grams, a bunch of kids showed up smoking weed, you know, marijuana. I just couldn't go there, either. I would never put you through that again or subject myself to either substance. Once I knew it was time for me to leave, Nick was already too high to drive. I drove his car here. Two of his friends were nice enough to follow me in their car, and then, one drove Nick home."

Ruby waited to make sure her granddaughter had finished speaking. "Evangeline, I'm proud of you." She paused, "Your grandfather would have been very proud, as well."

E.V. stood up and then bent down to hug her seated grandmother. "I miss G-pa a lot. Thanks for being so supportive, Grams."

The two released their embrace, and Ruby rose from her chair. "I miss him too, Eves. Wait here, please." The woman went into her own bedroom and returned a few minutes later. "I was saving this for your graduation, but now is a perfect time."

She handed E.V. a rectangular shape, covered in an old cloth and tied with a thin, faded ribbon. "What is it?" E.V. enquired.

Ruby responded with a quietness her granddaughter hadn't expected, "That happens to be your mother's diary. The wrapping is a piece of worn fabric that was Bonnie's favorite baby blanket for years until she outgrew it and out used it," Ruby smiled. E.V. was silent, so the grandmother continued, "I was waiting for you to graduate, but now seems to be an appropriate time. After all, what if something were to happen to me before then?"

"Grams, how could you even say that? You're still young and healthy!"

"Eves, regardless, it just wouldn't be a proper way for you to receive such a treasure." Ruby paused in obvious reflection. "Evangeline, I never, ever read your mother's journal. That just wouldn't have been right. Now, it's yours to do with as you wish. Please honor the poor woman's memory." E.V. just nodded. The two wished each other sweet dreams and a peaceful night.

Once E.V. readied herself for bed, she slid under the crisp sheet and old bed spread. She didn't turn off the light on her nightstand. E.V. bared the book from its soft covering and set the latter next to the lamp. The little locking mechanism was no longer held fast by its tiny key. E.V. simply slid the small metal release button to one side, and it immediately unlatched without resistance. E.V. withdrew the bronze-colored clip that had fixed the small strap over the pages for years. She touched the leather strip and wondered how many times Bonnie's own hands had completed the very same action. The book was opened. E.V. inhaled and held a short breath; she desired to ingest her mother's written voice in small, short sips. Evangeline ran her fingers along the thick, blue ink and imagined that she could feel the letters while she sniffed the pages to inhale her mother's words, her presence. She took in the first written entry and never noticed as the exhaled air passed through pursed lips:

Dear Diary,

Happiest Sweetest Sixteen to me! The party was good! My folks tried to stay out of the way. After we ate cake, which Momma did a great job baking, we went to the lake! I was kissed by boy number one and then, boy number two. Oh, yeah, then I kissed boy number three. Boy, oh boy, oh boy! No names to protect the not-so-innocent. Ha-ha! Of course, my girlfriends all kissed boys, too, well, except for Mary Ann. She wanted to go home early. I should have known ...

Evangeline read on. She learned from an entry that in the photo of her mother on the beach, Bonnie was in fact, pregnant! She was younger than E.V.'s present age. Years were unraveling like a spool of kite string caught in gusty winds. E.V. had to put the diary down. It was too much for a first glimpse into her mother's past. Bonnie's daughter had transitioned from having almost no history to knowledge of intense personal exposure. E.V. had the feeling that she was spying on a shadow of her mother's life. She shut the book with a determined motion and set it on top of the baby blanket remnant. E.V. thought it would have been difficult to fall asleep, until the sun peeked through her bedroom blinds the next morning.

She stumbled into the kitchen, and Ruby greeted, "How's it going, Eves?"

The teen's same response had been muttered many a time, "Okay, I guess. Hey, Grams, I don't feel much like going to church."

"That's exactly why you should go, E.V." The girl's silence was broken by Ruby's voice, again, but it was softer, "Dr. Davis suggested just the two of you meet, you know, to help her to help me. It could be perfect timing for you as well."

E.V. sighed with indifference, "Maybe."

Chapter Seven
WELL, WHAT DO YOU KNOW?

The reverend began the service almost the same way he did each Sunday with one exception. He asked everybody to refer to a printed sheet for the opening song instead of citing a page number in the hymnal. Then, he introduced guest musicians who stood up from the first pew and took their places at the front of the sanctuary where their musical instruments had been set up. Next, the minister introduced Pastor Dave Marshall to the congregation.

"We thought we'd do something a little different this week," he began. "To incorporate the spirit of ecumenism, Pastor Dave and his worship team from our neighboring church family will be leading today's service. That being said, tonight, yours truly will be the guest speaker at Pastor Dave's church. Maggie, our beloved organist, has the morning off but will provide the musical accompaniment this evening," he smiled. "Oh, yes, and please stop by for coffee, juice, and donuts in our fellowship hall after the teaching of the Word."

E.V. could only stare, at least until the worship and praise music began. Even Grams was swaying to the beat. After a powerful message from Pastor Dave, E.V. and her grandmother turned to one another. At the same time, they asked, "Want a donut?" They both giggled. Pete and E.V. immediately caught each other's eye. Over the promise of donuts, E.V. introduced both Pete and his dad to her grandmother.

Ruby shook their hands. "Thank you for staying with Evangeline until I was able to sign her out after that festival fiasco."

"It was our pleasure," Dave added. "I take it, we'll just see what the school administration has decided about clubs."

Ruby also thanked the two for the teaching and proclaiming of God's Word, accompanied by wonderful worship and praise music. E.V. echoed her grandmother's sentiments, shook both gentlemen's hands, and left with Grams. As they got into the car, Ruby let out a, "Well, what do you know?"

"About what, Grams? I don't think I studied for that test."

The older woman smiled as she looked over her shoulder and backed the car out of the church parking lot. "It's just an expression, Eves, but coincidences do seem to be slapping us upside our heads," she laughed. Over lunch, E.V. and her grandmother planned details for a get-together to celebrate the teen's eighteenth birthday. After that, E.V. cared for her pets and got caught up on her homework but not before reading a few more entries in Bonnie's diary. E.V. was surprised that Bonnie had written about her goal of becoming a nurse. It was the only ordinary thing Evangeline had ever associated with her mother. E.V. had known for years that she and Bonnie were very different.

The next day at school, Nick stopped by E.V.'s table in the cafeteria. There was very little small talk. Then, he began, "E.V., Friday night didn't go exactly the way I had planned. I just wanted to say, I'm sorry."

She almost responded that she believed it went exactly the way he planned it, but instead, shared, "Hey, Nick, we've had some good times, but this is just not going to work."

He stood up to leave but not without adding, "Well, sure it can, E.V. You're so pretty and smart and cool. The only thing adding a wedge between us is that you won't do drugs."

She was relieved that he did not visit her locker at the end of the day. After that, E.V. saw Nick as little as she had before they met. He didn't eat lunch in the cafeteria. They had zero classes together. The frequenting of her locker was a thing of the past.

E.V.'s birthday was the following weekend. She invited Emma, Destiny, and Scarlett over. She had considered asking Millie but decided it would just be too awkward. The gathering was pretty laid back, just the way E.V. had wanted it. Ruby stayed inside for most of it.

Grams was not expecting Nick to be at the door. He showed up with flowers, a box of chocolates, and a homemade card. Ruby stared at the young man as if she had missed the punch line to a bad joke. She asked him to wait, stepped out to the backyard, and beckoned E.V. to come inside the house. She whispered the situation to her grand-daughter, who then made her way to the front door. There was quiet small talk, and E.V. invited him in. She led Nick to the party out back as she continued to wonder how he would have known. Her mind was racing. Was he in communication with her friends? E.V. was only on limited social media. Nevertheless, she knew exactly what it felt like to be regarded as an outsider, and she despised that treatment.

The three girls noticed the newcomer and looked back and forth at each other to demonstrate their equal surprise. Not one to mince words, E.V. quietly took the boy aside and asked what he was doing at her house. His response was simple and loud enough for all to hear, "I made something for you, E.V." Nick set the flowers and candy on a picnic table. He held the card up to her. The picture on the cover was his finished drawing of the two of them dancing. E.V. took a breath. The artwork was stunning. Inside, the lettering read, "I'm glad we've met. Your friend, Nick."

Still, she pondered, his appearance was unannounced. Was it just an awful coincidence? She also thought she was clear about them not being in a relationship. Nick studied her expression and indicated that he had just come as a friend and nothing more. E.V. was still uncomfortable with the surprise. "Now that you're here, Nick, please join us," she offered.

During the celebration, Uncle Brad drove up in a ten-year-old European sedan. Ruby had purchased the gently used vehicle as a surprise for E.V. Brad walked into the kitchen, "Ma, I parked the you-know-what in the driveway." After a whisper from his mother, Bradley went to the backyard, wished his niece a happy birthday, pulled Nick aside, and from what E.V. later heard, had a man-to-man talk with him.

Bradley interjected, "E.V., why don't you and your friends meet us out front in say, five minutes." She looked at him with doubt and nodded with a shrug. Her uncle walked inside the house.

Ruby met her son as he quickly reentered the kitchen, "Bradley, that was a very considerate thing to do for Evangeline. I watched you and the boy talking."

"Thanks, Ma. The kid said that he and E.V. were just friends. Hey, we should get out front before E.V."

Moments later, E.V. invited her guests to exit the yard by way of the side gate. They moved to the opposite side of the house where Ruby and Uncle Brad were waiting. It took E.V. a minute to realize what had happened and cautiously exclaimed, "So, whose car?" The invited guests and one uninvited visitor looked around and shrugged.

Ruby and Bradley eyed one another. The matriarch spoke, "Yours, dear."

"Wha—what do you mean?" E.V. hesitated.

Uncle Brad held out a set of keys, "Here you go, kiddo."

E.V.'s caution merged into excitement. She opened the driver's door. "Can I; I mean, may I? I mean, thank you! It's amazing!"

"I'm surprised that you and your friends haven't already gone for a joy ride!" Grams couldn't contain her own enthusiasm.

The teens piled into the vehicle. One was eating a cupcake. E.V. specified, "Oh no, no food in my new car!" The girl popped the rest of the treat into her mouth before she entered. "That's better," E.V. chimed with a full-toothed smile. "Come on, Nick! Are you waiting for an invitation this time?" They all laughed at the obvious.

"Hey Eves," Grams poked her head through the open window and pointed at her granddaughter's seat belt. The teens all took the hint and a series of clicking sounds ensued. Then, the car pulled away.

Bradley broke through the air of exuberance with a serious demeanor, "Want me to follow them?"

"Nah, they'll be fine. E.V.'s in charge, and she won't mess up." Ruby sounded nonchalant yet confident.

Once the teens got back to the house, gifts were exchanged before E.V.'s guests departed. Ruby, Bradley, and E.V. went into the backyard to clean up. Uncle Brad told E.V. and his mother, "I set the expectations very high for that boy."

"Thank you, Uncle Protector," E.V. blurted out.

Bradley quipped, "Very funny, E.V."

"No, I really meant that," corrected E.V. "It was supposed to be taken to show my appreciation. Nick's okay, but he's figuring stuff out."

Ruby was astonished that her son had stepped forward. She patted him on the shoulder. Before E.V. tied up the last trash bag, she threw her arms around her grandmother's neck. "Grams, that was the most thoughtful gift, ever! Thank you! And thank you, Uncle Brad for bringing the car over."

That evening, E.V. read a few more entries from Bonnie's diary. She was surprised to learn that when the young woman got her driver's license, neither parent would allow her to have a car. They cited, "Irresponsibility and immaturity," according to Bonnie's writings. Wow, E.V. thought; Grams and G-pa Bill always said they were too lenient with Bonnie and Uncle Brad. In silence, E.V. decided to count her blessings.

The next week at school was tumultuous. There were two pop quizzes and an announcement sent home that some of the after-school clubs were suspended until further notice, which included the Christian Club. E.V. was furious. During her lunch break, she headed directly to the principal's office and demanded to speak with the administrator. When notified that the woman was busy, E.V. told the administrative assistant that she'd wait.

Finally, the assistant principal stepped out of his office and greeted the high school senior, "Come in, Evangeline."

E.V. was direct, "Mr. Jenkins, if the principal cannot join us, then we need a guidance counselor or other school official, present. I have to make a report." Two adults and E.V. then entered the inner office. "Mr. Jenkins," E.V. began, "the Christian Ministry Club has been canceled."

"Just suspended, Evangeline. That was where eye witnesses stated the trouble began. With all due respect, Evangeline, was that the club you attended?"

"No," she replied.

E.V. presented her testimony to the school officials. She had watched the story unfold at the Christian Youth Ministry booth. However, she also attested that there were other individuals from outside the school who added insulting assaults that led to violence. When that foreign group began to arrive, E.V. clearly viewed a man, who appeared to be in his late twenties, flash several crude gestures toward the band members. He threw two open water bottles, each filled with what appeared to be pebbles, at the musicians. No one else had reported that detail.

The assistant principal asked E.V. if she would give her statement to the police. She consented. The guidance counselor took notes as did the vice principal. E.V. was informed that she would be called back once a representative from the sheriff's office was available.

E.V.'s lunch break was clearly over by the time she left the front office. She hurried to class but needed to stop at her locker for her afternoon courses. She was startled to see Nick, busy in front of the locker. He was sliding papers between the slats. I'll deal with that later, she thought and proceeded to class without her materials.

Before the day had ended, E.V. was called to the office. A deputy was waiting for her. The two moved into a conference room adjacent to the front office. Shortly thereafter, the principal joined that meeting. After providing her testimony, the deputy handed E.V. his card in case she needed to reach him.

Before E.V. went to her car that afternoon, she stopped at her locker. Upon opening the metal door, Nick notes, as she called them, fluttered to the ground. Most of the small papers were blank. One had Nick's name on it and another had hers. There were a few cute cartoon-like figures, but none of the drawings made sense to E.V. On her way to the parking lot, E.V. dumped the papers into the receptacle at the end of the hallway where she exited the building.

That night, while E.V. was washing the dinner dishes, she looked over to her grandmother, who was packing up the leftovers for another meal. E.V. had not paid attention to how much Ruby had aged. It wasn't just her face but in her movements. The young woman absorbed it all and wondered whether Grams would have stayed physically younger had she not lost her daughter and more recently, G-pa Bill. E.V. sighed and even pondered how her own presence might have tacked on the years for her grandmother.

"Grams?" E.V. questioned.

"Mm-hmm?"

"I've put out some feelers for babysitting, you know, to pay for gas and insurance for Mimi."

"Mimi?" Ruby was clearly amused. "What a fun name for your car, Eves!"

E.V. chuckled, "Well, it's been in the family for a long time. Hey, Grams, what would you think if I started going to Pastor Dave's church? You can come, too!"

Ruby explained that she was sort of set in her ways about church. However, she pointed out that Evangeline Gold was of age, had her own vehicle, and as long as she was going to a Christian church, Grams would be okay with it. "Just be careful with that boy, Pete."

"How's that, Grams?"

"Are you and Nick still seeing each other, Eves?"

"Grams, that was way beyond done before my birthday. Nick just didn't get the little sticky note until Uncle Brad spoke with him," she smiled on the outside, but her insides felt twisted. She still hadn't made sense of the latest locker memos. "I think the roasting timer had already popped out on that turkey! Anyway, I'm not going to the church to see Pete." She interrupted herself, "Well, maybe I'm a tad interested, but I also like the teachings his dad offers as well as the worship music. Pete invited me to go to the student-led prayers at the flagpole each morning before first period. I went today. There were a few kids I'd seen before, and Nick wasn't there," she tipped her head to the side in victory.

During the same week, the school announced that the board made their decision over the protests that had occurred during the festival. All those involved who were not arrested owed the school service time. E.V. wondered whether her testimony helped, hurt, or had any impact at all.

All the implicated club members were asked, which E.V. considered a loose term, to create backdrops for an end of semester school play. Their volunteer labor would help cover the damages caused during the festival. E.V. already had a knowing about the school getting sued. One student was injured as she resisted arrest. A teacher fell and broke a wrist after being knocked to the ground in the skirmish.

The school decided a plan needed to be put in place to not only avoid such an altercation in the future but to negatively reinforce such aggressive behaviors on campus. They had the names of all students who were either arrested or needed to wait to be signed out by a parent or guardian that night. The administration had also arranged for counselors to be available the following Monday morning in order to provide comfort to all. E.V. later shared her opinions with Ruby, "Those teddy bear and bonbon cozy services cost big bucks but not as much as getting sued."

Chapter Eight

DONE!

It didn't appear as though the Christian Club would resurface during night school, at least during that year. As much as E.V. loved her evening art class, she was no longer interested in being in the same space as Nick. She had also connected with a few families from church and was babysitting after school and during some evenings. E.V. used the term, oxymoron, in regard to being forced to volunteer for the play. However, she did meet some interesting people via the experience. Nick, having remained at the art booth before he left with his mom and sisters on that night, was not part of an accused group. Pete, like E.V., had to be present to work with the play production team. E.V. considered that to be a plus.

E.V. had begun to attend the church where Pete's dad was pastor. Being able to meet Pete every weekday morning at the flagpole was good. They laughed easily together. Even when the group prayed for serious concerns, the students were lighthearted and filled with joy.

There were so many students who were forced to complete the in-school service project that there was talk of them being divided into days and shifts. When E.V. and Pete heard that, they both hoped to be chosen for the same time slots. Pete suggested the two pray about it. E.V. half-jokingly scoffed and said that prayer was only for serious intentions. Pete asked where in the Bible she had read that. E.V.'s quick comeback questioned where in the Bible it said prayer could be for requests of little importance.

Pete responded, "In John 14:13-14, the Word of the Lord states, 'Whatever you ask in my name, I will do it, that the Father may be glorified in the Son; if you ask anything in my name, I will do it.' Evangeline, Jesus said, 'If you ask anything.'"

Pete held out his two open hands in front and toward E.V. She complied, although she wasn't sure what she had just agreed to. Their hands met and felt warm and comfortable together. "Evangeline, in the name of Jesus Christ, we ask that the Father's will be done in positioning the two of us to work the same shift on the play production so that our Heavenly Father may use the two of us to do even greater works together than alone."

"Amen," E.V. affirmed.

Pete concluded, "Amen."

After dismissal the next day, all the volunteers showed up backstage. There were so many students that the teacher-coordinator asked them to move into the auditorium. The teens were divided among groups based on preferences they had filled out on note cards the previous day. Names were read. When both Pete and Evangeline's names were called for group B, Pete pointed to the ceiling and then gave a thumbs-up to the Lord. Evangeline looked down with a smile and shook her head back and forth. As groups were assigned tasks, E.V. laughed quietly and whispered to Pete that it was just a coincidence. "Correction, Evangeline, there are no coincidences with God," he smiled. She liked Pete's easy-going confidence.

They began to work on painting backdrops. To E.V., it was art. Mrs. Connor, the teacher, moved from group to group. She seemed to sense there was more to Evangeline Gold than the young lady permitted others to see. During the following meeting, the teacher told Evangeline that she suspected the student had a great business mind. Mrs. Connor suggested E.V. investigate the Teen Leadership Club. E.V.'s look made it clear that she was clueless about such a group. The performing arts production teacher explained that it was a lunchtime club designed for like-minded students. Twice a week, they'd bring food and gather in a computer lab to discuss and practice online gaming techniques that could be applied to future entrepreneurial endeavors.

The spark was visible on E.V.'s face, and the fire of her focus ignited. She asked about the days and times of the meetings and noted them on her cell phone. "Mrs. Connor, how do you know so much about that club?"

"Well, Miss Gold," the woman raised her eyebrows and offered a smile, "my son has been a devotee and my husband, Mr. Connor, happens to be the instructor."

E.V.'s grin revealed it all. That night, she was excited to share the newly proposed information with her grandmother, although E.V.'s mind had already been made up. She felt accomplished in her decision. After E.V. spoke at a more rapid rate than usual, her grandmother remained pensive for a few moments.

"Look," Ruby was tense, "you did not take pre-college board exams during your junior year due to the pandemic. You decided not to even attempt them in your senior year, so what are your plans, Evangeline? I don't understand where this is going."

E.V. replied to Ruby's cynical tone, "I might start at a local junior college, if I attend at all. I'm a train on a very purposeful track. I see no reason to stop at every station. You just can't see which direction I'm moving in, and it upsets you."

Grams pondered that she had inched along her own track toward a station titled, Exploration Exasperation. "You've had a close call with the law, a loser boyfriend, and to me, your future is not looking much brighter, E.V. What are you trying to prove?"

E.V. exhaled with a huff of air, "Nothing. I have nothing to prove nor anyone to prove it to." It was then that the girl saw Gram's woundedness and was brought back to the reality that she was not speaking to one of her peers.

Deflated, Ruby responded, "You have nothing to prove to me, E.V. I love you."

"I love you too, Grams." E.V. put an arm on her grandmother's shoulder.

"E.V., I don't want you to get hurt; that's all. I'm done with this conversation but am always available for you."

"Okay, Grams."

"Oh, I made an appointment with Dr. Davis. It's tomorrow after school. You could drive there yourself, or we could go together."

"I'll meet you there, Grams. Headed to my room to study unless you need anything at the moment." The older woman indicated with a shake of the head that her granddaughter was free to go. They hugged goodnight.

E.V. made her way to the bedroom and was sure to close the door before she opened Bonnie's diary. A little more than halfway through the two-year span of her mother's narrative, E.V. read and then reread the sentence, "I'll name her Samantha if she's a girl and Sam if I have a boy. I guess I'll be showing before summer vacation!"

E.V. flipped the pages back and forth in search of a hint. No way, she thought and slowly moved her head from side to side. "Well, I'm shook up," she let out a whispered breath. The next paragraph was about Bonnie's friends, Lucy, Tanya, Gayle, and one named, Bob. That might have been him, she thought. E.V. had never heard the name. Her mind raced. She actually didn't know her own father's name. She had referred to him as D.D., which stood for DNA donor. It was the impersonal way she named him, years before. E.V. never used an endearing name like dad or daddy. He remained unmentioned in the Gold household. In the diary, Bonnie talked about a summer job, going to the movies, and hanging out at the beach with friends but no further mention of a child or even a Bob for that matter.

E.V. continued to ingest the words. At the bottom entry, two pages ahead, Evangeline Gold read, "No Sam, no Samantha, no baby clothes, no lullabies, no growing belly will ever come to be. Thanks, almost-astronaut Mom."

E.V.'s eyes gaped opened so wide that she never even attempted to stop the tears that overflowed and streamed hot and salty down her face. I never expected that, thought E.V. and once again, she reread the words, sure that she had misread the content. "Grams!"

Within minutes, there was a knock at the door before it opened. "Did you call, Eves?"

"Um, oh, Grams, I just wanted to apologize for my tone, earlier."

"Me, too, E.V. I only want what's best for you."

"I know, Grams. Have a sweet night."

The next afternoon, E.V. found herself seated in a comfortable chair in the office of Dr. Davis. After the initial introductions, E.V. asked if it would be all right to switch to a love seat with plush pillows. "Of course, Evangeline. Make yourself right at home." The woman had a friendly smile that put E.V. at ease. "How are you, Evangeline?"

"I'm fine, Dr. Davis, but thought we were here to discuss Grams. Oh, I mean, Ruby Gold."

"Definitely, but if you have questions or if there is anything you'd like to discuss, go right ahead."

"I'm fine," E.V. nodded.

Dr. Davis asked E.V. how she would describe herself first, when she was an elementary school-aged student and then, as a teen. E.V. offered that she was a quiet, introverted child who liked to sit at home and read books. Later, she practiced the piano and violin for hours. She also mentioned her love of horses and household pets and how they had always given her satisfaction over the years. As a teenager, E.V. characterized herself with one word, independent.

The psychologist also asked E.V. to describe her Grandma Ruby. The words flowed, which surprised the teenager. "Grams has always been smart, caring, and sometimes, remorseful." Dr. Davis asked E.V. why she felt her grandmother might have been remorseful.

E.V. was quick to respond, "Not being on the Challenger craft; having been too permissive with Bonnie and Bradley, and just being lonely due to the loss of her husband. Dr. Davis, I've never thought that my grandmother would have been sorry that she and my grandfather had to raise me."

"Why would you bring that up, Evangeline?" Dr. Davis gently pressed.

The girl hesitated. She instantly sensed that her emotions had just spoken and driven home her intimate feelings about what she read the prior evening. After a long pause, "Well, you know, not everyone wants to raise another child once they've gotten older."

"I see. Thank you, Evangeline. There is one more thing, if I may ask. If you could give your grandmother anything, what might that be?"

"That's easy. I'd want Grams to have time with all her loved ones she has lost, even if it was for just one more day with each of them."

"Thank you, Evangeline. That may be the most honest and compassionate sentiment I've ever heard in all my years as a therapist."

"May I go now?" E.V. requested. "I have a babysitting job in an hour." Both doctor and E.V. stood, shook hands, and shared their appreciation in helping Ruby.

E.V. began to enjoy the play rehearsals that were ongoing as the set-creating team worked backstage. E.V. felt more comfortable around the crew than the cast. They had more similarities than she would have guessed. At first, she wanted nothing to do with the actual project. Connections continued. One artist dressed similarly to E.V. Others looked like regular kids, as E.V. categorized them. One girl's wardrobe reminded E.V. of a pioneer from the log cabin days. Of course, she and Pete also appreciated spending more time together.

During an afternoon, while E.V. and Pete were carrying a frame that would hold a painted scene, he invited her to join the worship band at his church. Although E.V. was flattered, she asked Pete how he could have asked, never having heard her play an instrument or sing. He looked surprised, "Evangeline, you're always singing as we paint and work, and yes, your voice is beautiful. I figured if you've dedicated so many years to your playing, you're probably pretty good. Plus, our keyboardist recently moved away, and you play piano. We would love a violinist, too!"

She only responded, "Thanks, and maybe."

At their first rehearsal, E.V. felt a bit unsure. Pete apologized for not praying before they began. He cleared his throat and admitted to being a bit distracted by the new musician. E.V. felt her face and neck redden, which she made a mental note of because it rarely happened. After working on the keyboard, E.V. brought her violin out from its case. She tuned up as the group was looking over the music and its recommended parts. Pete asked E.V. to start the instrumental intro. She played the piece cold, and the other band members stared. They were mesmerized.

After their practice session, Pete asked, "Evangeline, how did you learn to play like that? I'm so impressed."

"Thanks," E.V. quickly moved on to get past the uncomfortable feeling of being bragged about. "I was raised by my grandparents. They always said I needed to learn how to play at least one musical instrument, so I started piano at five. The violin came a few years later. My grandfather would always say, 'Reading and singing music unlock parts of your brain while your hands are working other parts in playing the instrument.'"

"Hmm, it's true," Pete contemplated. "I've never thought about music quite like that. And you sing."

She shrugged, "A little."

The next afternoon, E.V. attended the Teen Leadership Game Planners Club during lunch. She was surprised to see Callista, Millie, and Frederick there. Oh no, she thought, I hope Nick is not part of this. Pete also thought he'd give it a try. After E.V. introduced herself to Mr. Connor, she introduced Pete to the three students she already knew. By the middle of her first session, she had picked out the Connors' son. His name was Elijah. E.V. never considered herself a gamer but had to admit that the business slant made for a very intriguing forty-five minutes.

They logged out of the devices and were dismissed. E.V. and Pete were laughing as they walked through the door and into the hallway.

Nick stiffly stood at attention. E.V. nodded toward him and deducted that he was waiting for his three friends.

As E.V. and Pete walked away together, Nick suddenly turned around 180 degrees and began to follow the two. E.V.'s knowing took over. She spun around and shouted, "What?"

Nick stopped abruptly. "What are you doing with him?"

"Excuse me?" Evangeline Gold was not amused.

"E.V.," Nick appeared overwhelmed, "I brought you flowers, and candy, and the drawing was from my heart!"

He was beginning to sound whiny to E.V. "And that was all very thoughtful, Nick. But flowers just add sneezes for some. Yes, you heard me: irritating, itchy, loud sneezes."

"Well, Emma told me ..." his voice trailed off. "Oops, never mind," Nick stumbled over his own words and thoughts.

Pete stepped forward and positioned himself in between Evangeline and Nick. E.V. whispered, "Emma, of course, it was Emma." She raised her voice so both Nick and Pete could hear, "Look, Nick, you're fine; but we, we are done."

Nick looked down, "Then, I'll be done, E.V."

CHAPTER NINE

INSTANT GRATIFICATION

E.V. forced her eyelids to open. The bedroom was dark. The sun had not yet risen. The dream was so real that she didn't want to close her eyes for fear that she would go back to sleep and dream it again. Still, it replayed over and over again in her mind.

She was chained to what felt like either a concrete or an icy, rough stone wall. It was too dark to decipher any visual details. She heard moans and cries of others, both near and far. E.V. tried to break free, but the metal links were too heavy, too cold, too tight. Her wrists and feet were held fast.

The next day after school, during production work, E.V. shared the dream with Pete. He took out his cell phone and typed in a few words. "Evangeline, that sounds like Jeremiah 50:33."

"What does it say?" She looked puzzled.

Pete continued, "It's where the Lord explains in the Old Testament that the people of Israel and Judah were oppressed. 'All who took them captive have held them fast.' But the very next verse reads, 'Their Redeemer is strong; the Lord of hosts is his name.'"

"Well," she began slowly, "I don't feel like a captive."

"That's good," Pete acknowledged. "Maybe, ask the Lord what he wants you to know about the dream."

She stopped applying broad brush strokes and turned toward Pete, "How do I ask the Lord?" The two were working on painting large wooden forms that would be used on set. E.V. was enjoying her service. It provided time to use her creative talents and learn more about Pete.

He patiently responded, "You can simply ask him and listen. Some people journal, read Scripture, go on a prayer walk, or spend time in their prayer closet."

"I have lots to learn, Peter Marshall," E.V. decided aloud.

He smiled, "That's a great place to start."

"How do you know so much about the Bible and ways of the Lord?"

Pete continued to paint, "Second generation pastor's kid adds something," he turned toward E.V. with a brief grin, then redirected his focus on painting.

"Wow," E.V. added. "Do you think you'll go into the family business and be the third generation of pastors?"

Pete was quick to answer, "Oh, probably, not."

"Then, what do you see yourself doing after high school?" E.V. casually interjected.

For the remaining hour, the two painted, moved stage props, and shared. Pete offered his plans to either attend college for a business degree or go to business school. He shared that he had already applied, been accepted to three within Florida, and needed to discern where the best fit might be. E.V. listened intently. Pete then asked E.V. if she wanted to talk about her family background and future plans.

E.V. began by explaining that she was raised by her grandparents. Pete had already been aware of that. What came next shocked the young man. E.V. briefly explained how Bonnie perished from a drug overdose. She watched the jolt enter into Pete's spirit and exit through his demeanor. E.V. assured him that it wasn't such a big deal for her. After all, she was a toddler when it happened and had just turned three in time for the funeral.

"Evangeline, I'm so sorry!" Pete's eyes welled with water for a moment.

It was something E.V. had never experienced in a male counterpart. "Pete, I honestly only have a few memories. Losing my grandfather was a lot tougher. Before then, I thought it couldn't get any worse than when one of my best friends had moved away, and I wasn't allowed to buy his horse. Boy, was I wrong." Pete's quizzical expression coaxed more story from the young lady.

E.V. explained how during the summer before fourth grade, her grandparents enrolled her in a pottery camp held at the local community college. The plan was that she would attend with her friends. Young Evangeline learned about clay, wheel throwing, glazing, and more. Pete asked whether it made her think about God as the Potter while we are the clay. E.V. admitted that she never really understood that passage.

However, E.V. reminisced that she had been thrilled to take a summer course at a junior college. She and her best friend, Lisa, were going to be in the class together. However, when Lisa's parents changed vacation plans, E.V. went without her friend. She even asked Kristopher if he was interested, but he declined. The reasons he gave were being involved in practicing for and competing in horse shows and other sports.

"I remember back then, Pete. My grandmother was more upset than I was when she asked how I'd feel about taking the class with unknown kids. I really was okay with it. I was sort of a loner, anyway." He nodded and waited for more as he painted. "That summer, I created a ceramic Christmas ornament for Grams and G-pa Bill."

He continued to paint, "Evangeline, please tell me about your grandfather."

She spoke about him always being there for her. "He was a teacher by trade and loved sharing what he called, 'Real history lessons.'" E.V. added that G-pa Bill had been a veteran and believed in serving one's country. Her family often went to the beach and had fun together. E.V. was convinced that her life had been very good.

She related how that winter, between Christmas and New Year's, Grandpa Bill collapsed and was taken by ambulance to the hospital. E.V. admitted that she never quite understood it all until years later.

The tree and unopened gifts stood in memoriam of a time eternally changed by the turn of a page. Heart attack was a frequent word spoken by family and friends. E.V. remembered that she was unsure if that was the diagnosis for her grandpa or the bereaved, whose hearts had obviously been attacked and torn asunder.

All E.V. knew was that G-pa Bill was gone. Ruby talked dreamily about her husband being reunited with their daughter, Bonnie. That was completely intangible to young E.V. Bill was instantly gone, and no matter how many people assured her that she would see her beloved grandfather again, there was no way for E.V. to grasp those future details. She relayed that over time, she stopped believing the fantasy. Pete blinked hard at her interpretation of death.

She spoke about how strangers came and went. That time was difficult enough for E.V., but she made it clear that it was almost worse watching Grams deteriorate before her eyes. There were days when E.V. wanted to shake her grandmother out of the daze. In any case, E.V. was able to spend more time with Uncle Brad. As Ruby Gold finally seemed to wax back into the semblance of the woman everyone knew, the support of family and friends waned.

E.V. conveyed how she sensed a contrast when she returned to school after the funeral. Sentiments projected from teachers, acquaintances, and others had changed. School work was mostly completed. At home, there were no more history lessons, picnics, or trips to the beach. Even the backyard pool, a common feature to many Florida homes, was left unused. E.V. shared how her ceramic ornament sat somberly on the tree as a memento from the past that represented a tangible void in the future. Pete added nods and sounds of encouragement but the valve had been sprung, and E.V. continued her monologue.

"Instead, I dove into my music and art. Grams was mostly supportive as my hair, music, and clothing changed. I thought it best not to show my grandmother any more personal sketches that she referred to as macabre."

"I see," Pete added.

From fourth grade through junior high school, E.V. explained, she had two young people in her life who she considered to be friends. Kristopher owned horses, and he and E.V. would often ride. How she wished, as far back as she could remember, that she had her own horse. When Kris' parents decided to move to another state after eighth grade, E.V. mapped out a detailed scenario where she could buy one of his horses with money from her grandfather's inheritance. She offered to work to pay for food, board, and veterinarian bills. Ruby quickly put an end to the idea, but it was too late. E.V. told Pete she dreamed about, wrote in her journal, and sketched horses in a drawing book. She put money away each month to fund her goals. "Pretty silly, huh? Just little kid fantasies, I guess."

Pete encouraged, "Evangeline, dreams are never silly." Just then, Mrs. Connor made an announcement to clean up and put the supplies away for the evening. "I'll walk you out to your car, Evangeline Gold."

"Thank you, Pete Marshall."

Pete reminded E.V. to ask the Lord about the dream, and then wait and listen. E.V. nodded. She thanked him for hearing her story. He did the same. They both hugged before she got into her car. "Pete, you really did not tell me that much about yourself," she smiled.

"Well," he sighed and formed air quotation marks with his index and middle fingers of both hands, "our volunteer service hours are far from over." They both laughed.

Before she went to bed, E.V. asked God about her dream. She tried to stay awake but instantaneously fell asleep. In what seemed like only moments later, E.V. was crying out to the Lord. A chain broke off one ankle. E.V. was able to move around a little. She was cold. E.V. woke up, and her covers had slipped off the bed. She rearranged them and tried to go back to sleep. She looked at the time. There were still thirty minutes before her alarm would sound. She suddenly thought about Nick. E.V. was annoyed. She preferred to think about Pete. What did Nick even mean about being done, anyway?

At the end of the school week, Millie approached E.V. during their shared lunchtime club. "Hey E.V., some friends were wondering if you knew how Nick was doing. He hasn't been in school. He won't answer when we message him."

E.V. appeared surprised, "Why me? I mean, we aren't together."

"Okay, never mind. Just wondering," concluded Millie.

E.V. had decided to send Nick a message after school to check if he was all right. Once she left campus, E.V. typed, "Hey Nick, just checking in to see if you're cool."

The response was immediate, "This is Frances D'Angelino, Nick's mother. Stay out of his life! You've already ruined enough!"

Enraged, E.V. called Nick's phone number and instantly heard a frantic voice, "What have you done to my son?" the woman shouted.

E.V. was ready, "What have I done?" she yelled. "Look, I don't need him. Why would I? You're the one who needs your little boy and haven't yet figured it out. I mean, do you need the baby who once needed his mommy? He no longer exists. Or, do you need Nick, the little man who only needs his momma's pity? I'm certainly not her, but maybe, you are."

"You insolent ..." A stream of expletives came from the woman.

E.V. abruptly ended the call. She decided to call the police for a welfare check on Nick after his absences from school. It wasn't long before Frances called E.V., once again, screaming. From the mother's reaction, Evangeline was certain that Nick had taken his own life. The night before, she had a glimpse of an image of Nick on the floor of his room with an empty pill bottle on the nightstand.

After E.V. returned home from the horse farm, the next day, Ruby hollered for her to come to the front door. Someone was there to speak with her. A meticulously dressed police officer with fine features and her hair in a bun, stood straight and asked directly, "Evangeline Gold?" The girl nodded to hide the lump in her throat and tightening of her gut. "What do you know about Nick D'Angelino?"

She cleared her throat, "He's a troubled kid." E.V. silently deliberated and then decided against mentioning the alcohol from Nick's home that ended up at the beach. "I made a phone report to request that your department check up on him, not me."

The woman waited. "Evangeline, there has to be more. The boy's mother was not happy when a squad car showed up at their house."

"I already told you everything I know." The uniformed woman fixed her stare on the teenager, then Ruby, and settled back on the girl's face, once again. E.V. turned the question around and fired back, "If I were you and you were me, what would I be expecting you to say, officer?"

The deputy shook her head and looked back toward Ruby, who caught the rest of the burning glare. The policewoman spoke toward Ruby, "Ma'am, if you have any other information, here's my card and badge number. We are trying to help, and I'd appreciate a call. Good day." She pivoted and walked back to the patrol car. E.V. turned to face the bedroom hallway.

"Not so fast, missy," Ruby insisted.

E.V.'s eyes narrowed as she turned toward her grandmother. "He's just one more kid with problems, Grams. No big deal. He's apparently still alive and receiving help. The cop didn't say he was dead, and I saw him sprawled on a bedroom floor. Plus, his mother was none too thrilled to see the police, so Nick must be alive."

"You saw him, Eves?" Her voice became gentle.

"Grams, there was a knowing, and then I saw him. Like I said, he's getting help." The grandmother sighed, silently thankful that E.V. didn't divulge those details in the presence of the officer.

Later that evening, Ruby and E.V. came together for supper. "You know, Eves, I'm well aware that life is filled with complications for young people today. I would love to keep you protected in a little bubble, but that wouldn't be fair to either of us."

"I know, Grams. These days, everything happens so fast. G-pa Bill was here and then gone, almost instantly. Young people and even people like Frances D'Angelino can type messages and hit send or post without ever seeing the human being on the other side of the device. I got mad and screamed at her over the phone, and I'm sure she was hurting about her son. People can be so mean. Did Nick think about that bottle of pills for a long time or decide in a moment to try to end his life? Prescription drugs are quite available, and all it might take is for a kid not to get enough likes on social media. Priorities are messed up, Grams."

"I just don't know, E.V. The Challenger and crew also ended abruptly. I should probably write that in my journal and share it with Dr. Davis."

E.V. whispered, "journal" under her breath. It was the word that triggered the next outburst, "And why did you pay for my mother to have an abortion?"

Ruby was not shocked by the inquiry. "I was expecting that question, Eves. I couldn't imagine your mother omitting it from her diary. I thought I could protect Bonnie from embarrassment and provide a fresh start for her. She wasn't happy with me. I thought it was for the best," Grams shook her head.

E.V. saw the brokenness in the old woman. She stood up and walked around Ruby's chair. She gave her grandmother a hug. "I still love you, Grams."

Ruby patted E.V.'s forearm, "Love you too, Eves."

ON THE EDGE

Evangeline sat on the side of her bed. She opened an upright port-folio folder that leaned against the nightstand. E.V. drew out a piece she'd been working on during the evening art elective before she dropped the class. She studied the rainbow that was shaded in black and gray tones rather than the color spectrum. A broken and bleeding heart hovered above. Blood dripped the only colorful pig-ment from the top of the page and then burst forth from the arch in every direction with a crimson shower. Musical notes bulged and ballooned from the bow.

Above and to the right, a wooden-framed window stood apart from the rest of the drawing with the bottom sash opened. Below that image, there were two smaller drawings of the same window. One showed the perspective as if looking through from the inside. An adjacent sketch depicted the image of the same window as if the view was portrayed from the exterior of the ledge. A bright light shone against the glass but only on the outside picture. From the inside face of the window panes, light did not permeate the glass, even where the lower sash had been opened upward. From the internal view, the panes were dirty, smudged, and a crack ran through the upper portion. Spattered blood from the heart trickled downward inside the panes.

There was a bird shown from the inside window view. It was bound and lying on its side. One wing was partially exposed. The glass and inner ledge that the bird had been set upon were quite soiled, and the old paint was greyed and peeling. A giant pair of scissors seemed to float just above the bird and moved to cut the feathers on the side of its exposed wing. The creature had been pinioned so it would be unable to fly. E.V. often felt that she had clipped wings. She had recently realized that what felt like restraints were Gram's ways of protecting her. E.V. wanted to stop thinking about Bonnie's abortion, but it had become implanted deeply within her.

It was then, as she stared into her own work, E.V. realized that in her two dreams, she was pinioned to the wall. She wanted to read more of Bonnie's diary but was almost afraid to resume where she had left off. E.V. reminded herself that she didn't have many fears. The angst of what she might read next, made it difficult for E.V. to take a complete breath. Maybe I need more sleep, E.V. pondered in silence. I've been so tired, she reminded herself. She had to pry herself out of bed each morning.

The work with Pete became the highlight of E.V.'s week. As their friendship developed, she and Pete shared more and more. One afternoon, they reminisced about growing up in the same small town. Pete moved there in the fourth grade. They compared notes.

E.V. began, "I was in Miss Salter's class. What about you?"

"Same class, Evangeline."

"No way!"

"Uh-huh," he nodded, looked down for a moment, and then back up. "I remember you. Wait, you mean to say you don't remember me?"

She laughed, "I'm so sorry, Pete! I don't."

As the two assembled pieces of furniture for the play, they paused and prayed together for Nick. They had recently learned that Nick had been admitted to an adolescent unit of a mental health hospital. Pete stated, "You know, Evangeline, every time you spoke about Nick, you shared how relieved you were in the times when he wasn't present." E.V. had a puzzled expression on her face. Pete continued, "Examples of those instances were when he didn't show up somewhere or when

you didn't have to slow dance with him, and when he slept on the way home from that sad beach outing."

"Oh, no, Pete, that wasn't true." They both paused in silence. "Actually, yes, Pete, that was all true. You saw it first, and now I recognize it." He raised his eyebrows and gently smiled.

Pete looked around to ensure they were relatively alone. At least the hammering, talking, rehearsing, and moving of props created background noise. "Evangeline, would you like to join me, I mean, my family and me for an evening of prayer combined with a Christian concert? It's at the end of the month at our church. Oh, and of course, your grandmother is invited too!"

"I've never been to either but sure, I guess so. Thanks for asking." E.V. looked down for a moment and then up at Pete, "I think I'm supposed to go." He nodded, and they went back to work.

During one of the afterschool play production work meetings, Meagan, one of the two girls who danced with the other female when the entire bad scene occurred at the festival, was placed in E.V. and Nick's group. Slowly, other students surrounded her with snide remarks and crude innuendos.

As they persisted throughout the session, E.V. was clearly fed up. "Hey, guys, knock it off, already!"

Another classmate joined in with a snarky tone, "How come, E.V.? Are you her girlfriend, too?"

Pete bristled but kept silent. E.V. was never fond of Meagan, but knew she was in no position to judge after all that she, herself, had been through. E.V. kept her voice down to avoid alerting Mrs. Connor and getting into trouble. Play production was one of the best things that had happened for Evangeline Gold in a long time, and she was determined not to ruin it. "Take your gender agendas somewhere else," E.V. growled in a low voice.

Mrs. Connor was suddenly standing in front of the group. "This is an official alert to each of you. One warning is your limit before this nasty little name-calling fest gets you suspended." She separated the angry group from one another, except for E.V. and Pete. Mrs. Connor had obviously been eyeing the cluster earlier and then moved in as tempers flared and reactions escalated.

After class, Pete walked E.V. to her car. "Wow, Evangeline, I've never almost gotten suspended!" he laughed.

"Very funny, Pete." She was still annoyed. "Some people assume they can just say any dumb thing to anyone they don't like. I'm in no position to pass judgment. Heck, I don't even like that girl I stood up for. It was just the point."

"That's one of the many things I like about you, Evangeline."

She looked down, unsure of what to say. "Hey, want to come for dinner at my house this weekend?"

"Sounds great!" he smiled.

"I'll talk to Grams. I think she'd like that, too."

They said goodnight, and E.V. drove home. When she entered the kitchen, Grams was sipping her customary evening cup of tea. E.V. told her grandmother about what had transpired that night.

"Well, child, it was very generous of you to stick up for that girl. Glad you didn't get a suspension, Eves. It would not have looked good on your record, especially just a few short months before graduation."

"Grams, it's not like I wake up every morning looking for a fight. They find me."

"Walk away, dear."

E.V. added, "There's a big difference between walking away and running away."

Grams humbled herself, "Can't argue with that, Eves."

The next day, during Ruby's appointment with Dr. Davis, they spoke about the Gold family's current events. "Well, Ruby, it sounds like there have been numerous positive changes."

"Doctor, I still think about Challenger, but it certainly seems farther away these days. Does that mean I'm getting dementia?"

"There are tests for that, Ruby, but at this time, I don't believe you are a candidate. Instead, I'd say that first, your granddaughter is growing up. Second, it sounds as if your son has also done some maturing of his own. And third, because you brought up those situations during our visit, they must be rather important to you."

"With Bill gone, Doc, I have no sounding board for raising E.V., you know, someone to bounce ideas off." Ruby continued, "Evangeline remains a headstrong young lady. However, she has used some of her gifts to make sound decisions. For example, she was working Saturdays on a horse farm to earn some extra cash. She now has a used vehicle to call her own and added babysitting jobs to raise more money. When she can fit it in, E.V. has taken on a few dog walking clients as well."

Ruby then mentioned, "E.V. ended a relationship with a confused high school boy who is now an inpatient in some kind of institution. I'd venture to say she found a new friendship with a young man who is a local pastor's son. Then, there was a school festival that had some unfortunate events, and E.V. almost got into trouble with the law. She's working off her punishment at the school, but thankfully, we didn't have to go to court."

"Ruby, I don't know what transpired on campus, but getting into some school trouble still sounds better than being charged or adding a criminal record," Dr. Davis encouraged.

Ruby nodded in agreement. "Doc, I gave Bonnie's diary, untouched, to Evangeline. To my knowledge, not a soul, except for Bonnie, had ever opened or read it."

As Dr. Davis spoke, she also jotted down notes. "How'd that go?"

Ruby mentally reassured herself about why she trusted, felt connected to, and held the psychologist in high regard. "After reading an entry, E.V. straight up asked me why I paid for my own daughter's abortion."

"How'd that make you feel, Ruby?"

"Dr. Davis, I'm not proud I did it."

"Did you let Evangeline know how you felt about funding the procedure?"

The aging woman paused as she thought, "No, I didn't. I just related that back then, I wanted to protect Bonnie from further hurt. E.V. doesn't know about my sentiments. I never told Bill, either." She reached for a tissue on the desk in front of her and wiped away a tear from below her eyeglass frames and then went on, "He never knew he lost a grandchild."

"Ruby, I would encourage you to have a frank conversation with Evangeline, explaining how you felt about your part in the abortion back then and your feelings, now. It's healthy to let young people see that our views can change over time. We can talk about Bill, separately."

"Good idea, Dr. Davis. It would probably do us both some good to air out that unmentioned past mistake."

When Grams arrived home, Evangeline's car was in the driveway. Ruby found E.V. napping in her room. The bedroom door was partly opened. As the woman approached, her granddaughter stirred and woke up. Ruby asked whether the girl was all right, since play production was scheduled that afternoon. E.V. told her grandmother that she was just very tired. Ruby understood. There was the afterschool service project, three part-time jobs, and school itself, although Ruby did not figure that E.V. had put much effort into the final factor.

E.V. rubbed her eyes and sat up. She told Grams that she had asked Mrs. Connor for permission to leave at dismissal instead of staying for the production work, because she was not feeling like herself. Mrs. Connor agreed but said it would be the only allowed absence without a note from a parent or guardian. Ruby nodded and decided to keep a closer eye on E.V.

Earlier, Pete had overheard the conversation with Mrs. Connor and later called E.V. to check in. E.V. assured him that she just had a lot going on and was simply tired. However, she did express her appreciation for his genuine concern. They spoke for almost an hour before Pete suggested that she get some rest. She apologized for not being there to help him with the sets. They said goodnight and made a plan to meet at the flagpole for prayer in the morning.

That next afternoon, Ruby received a call from E.V.'s guidance counselor. She asked the guardian to come in to meet. Ruby asked what E.V. had done and felt uneasy when the counselor shared that they first needed to speak in person and then have E.V. join them. Ruby said a prayer as she got into her vehicle. Once inside the counselor's office, she was told that E.V. was cutting.

Ruby's response was, "Who or what has my granddaughter cut?"

"Herself, Mrs. Gold."

The older woman could not make sense of the term. Some explanation was necessary on the part of the school counselor. It had been reported that E.V. had numerous scrapes on the inside of one forearm and both wrists. Some were barely scratches while others appeared to be deeper. Various scabs were almost healed while other incisions were fresher with pink marks surrounding them. Ruby stared in disbelief. The counselor further shared that E.V. did a good job covering up the damage by either wearing long sleeves or terry cloth wristbands.

"But why?" Ruby stammered.

"Mrs. Gold," the counselor calmly stated, "many students engage in such behaviors to force themselves to feel one type of pain in order to mask another. Cutting has also been a way for young people to release stress."

E.V. was called out of class. She was stunned to see her grandmother in the front office. "Grams, is everything okay?"

Ruby made her request with a quiet thoughtfulness, "Please tell me, Eves, why you are physically hurting yourself?"

The girl was surprised yet honest. "It relaxes me."

For the first time, the grandmother truly noted the dark terry cloth wraps on E.V.'s wrists. Ruby stared at the athletic sweatbands on E.V.'s arms and motioned her head upward and slightly to one side. E.V. immediately understood that it meant to remove the soft elastic covers. The girl pulled them both off and bared her wrists and fore-arms. Ruby looked away for a moment, then back at E.V., and then toward the counselor.

The three had a brief conversation and came up with some strategic interventions. The first was that Grams would set up an appointment with Dr. Davis. The counselor also offered a few exercises for stress relief. She asked E.V. if she would sign an agreement to receive help and not hurt herself further. E.V. shared that she had tried numerous times to end the behavior but always lapsed back. E.V. was embarrassed but also slightly relieved that someone had noticed and reported the marks.

The next morning, Dr. Davis met with E.V. When the assessment was over, she asked Evangeline's permission to call her grandmother in so the three of them could discuss the situation. The youth nodded twice in agreement.

Dr. Davis was matter-of-fact. "Cutting can be an attempt to open up and release stressors." The doctor nodded individually at both women, "Evangeline, Ruby, we can do the same, therapeutically speaking, and expect positive results through counseling. Of course, Evangeline, you would need to be open to the exercises and practice them outside this office setting as well."

E.V. rolled her eyes and sighed, "More assignments."

Dr. Davis acknowledged that it would take work. She explained that the act of cutting causes the individual committing self-harm to try and relieve the perception of trapped torment by opening the skin. The combination of Nick and his hospitalization, E.V. learning of her own mother's abortion, the entire unfair volunteer service, and how the school never admitted that outside forces played into the altercation on the night of the festival were all too much for her.

The girl wanted to return to school after the appointment. She felt compelled to share with Pete and bring darkness into the light. In the parking lot after school, E.V. had a cathartic discussion with Pete. He admitted he had noticed that she often wore long sleeves year-round, even though they lived in Florida. When she didn't wear long sleeves, Pete shared, Evangeline often had black terry cloth sports bands on both wrists. When he asked her about it in the past, E.V. had attested that the school's air-conditioning made her cold, hence the sleeves.

"Evangeline," he began, "I reported it to Mrs. Connor after I saw scratches peeking through."

She self-consciously checked the position of the terry cloth bands. "Are you kidding me?" her volume and pitch both increased.

Pete gently placed his hand on her arm. "I brought it up with you more than once, Evangeline. You clearly didn't want to discuss it." She leaned against her car, exhaled, and nodded. Pete offered his earnest advice, "Evangeline, cutting was a way to create covenant among the people of the Old Testament. If I may ask, who were you making a covenant or promise with?" Pete waited, and an abundance was spoken in the silence and downward shake of E.V.'s head. He continued, "You see, Jesus bled for each of us. There's no more need for anyone to bleed if we accept him into our hearts."

She took it all in to remember the words and sentiments, so that later, she could record in her journal what Pete had said. Yet, her only response was, "I have a dog-walking job to get to." Evangeline Gold got into her car and drove away, leaving Pete standing there, alone.

CHAPTER ELEVEN
HOMEWARD BOUND

Instead of Pete coming over by himself, a school group from the online business club arrived at E.V.'s house for pizza and a game night. Days before the pair's parking lot discussion about the cutting, E.V. and Pete had scheduled the gathering with Callista, Millie, Elijah, and Frederick. Being with Pete felt slightly awkward for E.V. at first, but then the two quickly warmed up. E.V. tried not to think or care about whether Elijah Connor's mom had let her son know about the cutting.

Grams stepped inside the kitchen to greet the guests. She put two slices of pizza and a serving of salad on a plate and then retired to the back patio with her food. E.V. excused herself and followed Grams outside with an iced tea. As E.V. walked back toward the house, she quickly and repeatedly snapped a rubber band that was fastened around her forearm. The purpose, according to Dr. Davis, was to release anxiety by sensing the sharp twinge without causing physical damage to oneself. It wasn't the same as cutting, but E.V. gave it a chance. When the teen returned to the kitchen, the young people commented that they thought it was cool that she was an only child and lived with an elderly lady. Hmm, quite the novelty, Evangeline silently acknowledged with the slightest external shrug.

The teens moved into the living room after dinner. They were surprised that E.V. didn't own a gaming console. She had taken out board games and classic team-based strategy matchups that hadn't been touched since G-pa Bill died. Some had been gifted to her and were still preserved within the original shrink wrap. E.V. was impressed with how intelligent the group was. They planned, laughed, and preferred the games where they could compete in teams. The concept of having new friends, or at least acquaintances, over to the house was novel to E.V.

When Ruby stopped by to check whether the guests needed anything, Pete offered her a prime spot at the coffee table to play. The others also encouraged the woman. Millie cajoled, "Join us, Miss Ruby." The grandmother chuckled, thanked the young people, and instead, decided to have a hot cup of tea before bed. Ruby reminded E.V. that she had baked cookies earlier in the day. When E.V. stood up to return to the kitchen for those treats, Pete followed her.

"Please, let me help," he offered. That sentence unblocked E.V.'s heart, which was laden with emotions, and she found herself filled with gratitude for the young man. Her eyes flooded with tears. Grams sensed the moment, excused herself, and left the room. Pete remarked, "I want what's best for you, Evangeline, and I want what God wants for you."

"What does that even mean?" she questioned him as much as herself.

Pete grabbed a stack of napkins while E.V. arranged the cookies on a plate. "The Lord has and knows his good plans for each of us, Evangeline. That's a rough translation of Jeremiah 29:11," he smiled. "Before we go back out there with those ruffians, I'd like to ask you a question." She nodded but felt herself stiffen. "Would you still honor me by going to the prayer night and Christian concert at the end of the month?"

E.V. let a sigh of relief slip out, "I'd like that, Pete."

He grinned, "Me too."

The following school week began at the flagpole. E.V. was stunned to see Nick standing there. E.V. had an uncomfortable feeling for a number of reasons. She stood next to Pete and as had become customary, they reached for the other's hand in prayer. After the students laid out petitions and praises of thanksgiving, the group disbanded to go to class. Nick passed by E.V. and Pete as he moved in the opposite direction. Nick nodded to the two. E.V. didn't react.

In a friendly tone, Pete greeted aloud, "Hey, Nick."

The twosome and Nick continued on their opposite trajectories. As Pete walked E.V. to her first period class, she whispered, "I hope he'll be okay. He's not a bad guy."

"Agreed. We'll keep him in prayer like we've done and continue to trust in the Lord."

Consistency became the elixir for E.V. Mornings in prayer at the flag pole led to a healthier outlook for the remainder of her senior year in high school. She worked for play production on the assigned days after school and also wedged in her three jobs. E.V. helped Grams where she could and still had her Saturday work at the horse farm. Sundays were for church. The worship group rehearsed their music before each service, so they'd be ready to make a joyful noise unto the Lord, as Pete often reminded them by quoting Psalm 98:4.

E.V. had put Bonnie's diary aside for a while. She felt it was her duty to process the journal but was no longer compelled to digest everything at once. It had already taken E.V. eighteen years to learn about a few small pieces of her mother's life. What difference would it make if she spent another eighteen to gain a personal glimpse of two partially-recorded years of Bonnie's experiences? E.V. decided to jump ahead and read the last page, which only promised, "Today marks eighteen years on this earth. With baby growing inside, I'll be starting a new diary real soon." It was signed, "Bonnie Lynn Gold."

E.V. had only sparse communication with Destiny and Scarlett since her birthday but none with Emma. She admittedly hadn't thought of them much with all that had been transpiring in her own changing life. She wasn't even sure what had made her think of the girls as she waited for Pete at the flagpole. Her hair was tied back in a ponytail as the Florida sun beat down. It was morning, but spring had already ushered in what E.V. called, the southern hot and humid. She saw motion toward the opposite side of the flagpole. E.V. briefly looked up and did a doubletake. There they were. Nick and Emma stood together, holding hands and ogling one another. E.V. tore her gaze away but couldn't help whispering, "Interesting."

Pete had just walked up next to E.V. with a few other students. "Good morning, Evangeline. What's interesting?"

"Oh, hi," she met Pete's eyes with a brief smile. E.V. then raised her eyebrows and nodded across from where they both stood.

Pete refrained from saying anything at first. "Bless them," he finally said in a quiet voice.

As they walked to E.V.'s first class of the day, she declared, "I can't believe it! Emma must have been the one who told Nick about my birthday."

Pete never missed a beat, "I really like your new short-sleeved blouse, Evangeline. It looks very nice on you. And what's that new fashion called, zero wristbands?" he playfully grinned with closed lips and his eyes smiling.

It made E.V. giggle as she thanked him for the compliment. She quickly caught on to what he was doing. However, E.V. thought it was sweet that Pete noticed she was no longer cutting, and her arms were healing. E.V. was also aware that Pete tried to avoid any gossip. She thanked him for noticing her new clothing, as well as offering the subliminal reminder not to talk about others, especially if unkind or unnecessary.

Theater production work was winding down. The students who had been working off their service hours were released from what E.V. termed, indentured servitude. Only a handful of volunteers remained. Pete and E.V. decided to pitch in and help. They enjoyed each other's company as well as the actual artistic labor. Plus, neither of them had the extra cash for expensive dates, so it was a way to increase their time together. They both made an effort not to use terms such as seeing each other or girlfriend and boyfriend. However, their relationship was obvious to everyone around them.

E.V. found Mrs. Connor to be fair as the program's coordinator. She was tough when necessary but also understanding. E.V. described her as steady. She liked that quality in an adult. E.V. figured that was how parents were supposed to be. The week before, Tammy Connor gave a talk in church about how to pray for spiritual protection. E.V. was surprised to see the Connor family at Pete's church. Elijah and his younger sister sat next to Wayne Connor while their mom spoke. Mrs. Connor also touched on a practice she referred to as discerning or distinguishing between spirits, referenced in 1 John 4:1. Evangeline was astonished that something as ethereal as the spiritual realm could not always be trusted. Tammy Connor drove it home with 1 Cor 12:10. She relayed that the enemy was on the prowl to kill, steal, and destroy, whereas Jesus came to lay down his life that we may all have abundant life. (John 10:10-11)

Wayne Connor, the computer teacher, was easygoing. E.V. and Pete still attended the online business club twice a week during their lunch time. E.V. found it relaxing to be around that group. She respected their intellect. She had even shared with Grams that the students were quiet, focused, and entertaining in a reserved sort of way. The teens tried to get together outside of school for game nights when schedules permitted. Their first get-together took place at E.V.'s house. After that, each took a turn inviting the group to his or her own home. A bond had formed. E.V. attended whenever possible and soon noticed that she was the only one in the bunch without numerous high-tech electronics in the home.

When they were all invited to Frederick's house, E.V. learned that he was a foreign exchange student from Canada. She recognized the high school students in the same home who, with their parents, made up Frederick's host family. They all ate together, but after the young people worked to clean the kitchen, the family's natural children went off to do something else. When Pete offered to help set up the games, he asked whether Frederick went by nicknames, Fred or Rick.

The statement was clear, "Neither, just Frederick."

They all learned so much more about their group of friends over suppers. Millie was being raised by an aunt. She had two cousins and one sister who also resided in the snug garden apartment. Her aunt baked homemade lasagna and bread and served a colorful salad with the meal. Callista shared that she also went by the name, Callie, which her father called her before his untimely death. She had the largest and most elegant home of the group. Yet she and her mom were down-to-earth. Elijah was easygoing like his dad, and E.V. had a deep respect for Mrs. Connor. E.V. was most impressed by how the group had fun whenever and wherever they were together. E.V. took it all in and for the first time, recognized that her family life was quite average when compared to others of similar ages. The week before the concert, Pete hosted a game night. He had two younger brothers, Joshua and Caleb, and an older sister E.V. had not yet met. While they ate sandwiches, he invited the group to the night of prayer and Christian music.

The following week, E.V. asked Pete what time she should meet him at the church for the special event. He said that he wanted to pick E.V. up at her house. He also mentioned that his mom was inviting her and Ruby to their home for dinner before they headed out. E.V. called Grams. Although Ruby graciously declined, she encouraged her granddaughter to go. E.V. let Pete know and said she would bake and bring chocolate chip cookies for dessert.

The concert was held in a large church, two towns away. When E.V. and Pete arrived, a backup band was playing instrumental worship music. Once the crowd assembled, pastors, youth leaders, visiting missionaries, and other speakers took turns on stage with inspiring messages and teachings. Pastor Dave gave a talk about hearing God's voice. Pete's mother, Janet, sat in the row behind them, along with the Connor family. After each speaker, the main band played one to two songs. During the praise and worship music, Elijah moved up a row to sit with Pete and E.V.

There were exercises in trust, suggestions on how to dive more deeply into Holy Scripture, and challenges to spend more time alone with Jesus, just allowing him to love each individual. After the lessons and sermons, the majority of the orators returned to the platform to pray over those in attendance. Prophetic utterances were also released. The headliner band took over. Music vibrated within E.V. She permitted it to take her to a new place. Most of the people were on their feet with arms outstretched to God.

E.V. sat down and then closed her eyes. Multiple images flashed before her. Good times, horrible memories, and some, which she could not even decipher, glued her eyes shut. She saw people in her life who had berated her from childhood up through the present. They yelled as one voice that demanded to know why she needed to be so different and would never give in to what they subscribed to as the norm.

Evangeline heard herself speak out, but it was within her own mind. "I am a warrior. That means I continue to stand and fight even after my heart has been shattered."

"You are a warrior for me, Daughter of the Great I Am."

E.V.'s eyes opened and darted rapidly about before she exhaled with a sharp breath. No one else in the group looked up, not even Pete, who stood next to her, singing lyrics projected upon large screens. The worship music continued. No, she reasoned, that was inaudible to the others in attendance. "Who are you?" she barely whispered. She suddenly remembered the instructions of Tammy Connor to discern the spirit. E.V. spoke up more boldly, "If you are not sent by The Father, his Holy Spirit, or Jesus our Lord and Savior, who bled, died, and rose for us, then in the mighty Name of Jesus, covered by his Precious Blood, I take authority over you. I bind and evict you far, far from here, far from our loved ones. Be nailed to the foot of the cross to be dealt with by Jesus Christ!" She felt a rumbling, a shaking in her essence, and then dropped to her knees.

"Evangeline, I Am God, the Three in One."

She knew. She trusted. She listened and then responded, "I am here to serve you, Lord."

"Daughter, Warrior, your heart has been broken. Allow me to mend and strengthen it. Now you fight for me. Take courage and discern. You are an important thread of my remnant."

"Yes, Abba, Father." She had never addressed anyone by either name. It was more than a title. It was a name, his name. E.V. suddenly reflected back to the pottery classes from her youth. She made a connection about the potter and the clay. She felt his presence working in, molding, and fashioning her. E.V. quietly asked, "Lord, how will I answer your call?"

"Spend time with me, my Word, and my children, your brothers and sisters."

The phrases were crisp and gentle within her heart. The shaking had stopped as abruptly as it had begun. Her eyes were closed, and she was still on her knees, hands folded, resting on the seatback of the chair in front of her. Suddenly, she saw an image. It was a very tall building. She could only view what she surmised were the top floors due to the perspective of surrounding sky. Dark clouds billowed around those floors and from below. A heavy shadow appeared above the edifice, encircling its circumference. Her brow furrowed, but E.V. dared not open her eyes. The building began to crumble from the top down. Simultaneously, a pristine metallic, glass-domed edifice took its place, replacing what was deteriorating below. Her vantage point broadened. Other new buildings, similar in construction, were being formed and positioned in what had been a large city. "I will rebuild it all for my children, because my remnant prayed."

One of the pastors in the room announced an altar call. E.V. remained at her place. She had never witnessed lines of people publicly giving their lives over to Christ. Finally, everyone was dismissed to go out and do the work of the Lord.

While Pete drove E.V. home that night, they spoke about the music, the talks, the altar call, and the atmosphere. The two shared their impressions. E.V had some questions that Pete answered openly and honestly. E.V. learned that Pete and his youth group had prayed for her without specifying her identity. They prayed that God would lift the veil and that Holy Spirit would be on the move.

"Thank you, Pete; you've been my rock," E.V. declared.

His grin came before the words, "That's what Jesus called Apostle Peter, you know, Saint Peter or Petros!"

"So many names?" E.V. enquired.

Pete was engaged, "In the Greek Translation of John 1:42, Kephas or Cephas was from the Aramaic word, Kepha. The first syllable is pronounced like your house key." They arrived in her driveway and talked some more. Finally, Pete walked E.V. up to the kitchen door. They hugged, and he gave Evangeline a quick but comfortable peck on the cheek.

That night, E.V. instantly fell asleep. However, she was awakened moments before 3 a.m. and actually watched the clock change. E.V. had just dreamt that she was situated back in the same environment as the two, initial similar dreams. E.V. heard herself cry out in reverence for the Lord. A chain from one wrist dropped off and a dim light enveloped the tiny area of what appeared to be a jail cell. Her ankle remained free. E.V. heard more cries that surrounded her. She woke up curious about the meaning for herself but deeply saddened for others.

Chapter Twelve
THERE'S WORK TO BE DONE

That next morning, Evangeline once again invited Grams to join her at church. E.V. told her grandmother that she wanted to share her personal feedback from the prayer meeting and worship concert. Grams agreed. E.V. was a little surprised the woman said yes but was looking forward to spending time together. On the way to church, E.V. spoke about her experiences from the night before. Ruby listened.

After the service, Ruby met with Pete's parents. She shared how impressed she was with Evangeline's hunger for the Lord. Janet complimented Ruby and her late husband for raising such a talented and spiritual young woman. Pastor Dave invited Ruby to attend their church anytime.

While the adults met, Pete took E.V. aside. "I have something for you."

"Oh?" E.V. asked.

Pete removed a small fabric bag from his guitar case. He opened the pocket-sized, cloth drawstring pouch and presented a bracelet to E.V. It was comprised of thin, braided strips of leather that came together in a knot. A proportionately-sized wooden cross was clasped to that point with a jump ring where the bracelet could be opened and closed. "May I?" he asked.

"Yes, please," E.V. smiled. She admired the bracelet but also studied the young man as he secured the clasp. "Thank you, Pete. You're so thoughtful."

Pete spoke while he attached the gift. "Just a little something to celebrate your hard work and determination. You have grit, Evangeline," he grinned. E.V. knew that he referred to the absence of cut marks on her forearms.

Once home, E.V. took out the drawing paper with her bleeding rainbow, as she termed the work. She began to add other colors to shade the area around the large drop of deep red blood that fell from the exhibited heart. E.V. used fine-point markers and inserted vibrant, falling liquid beads. She introduced new droplets onto the page so that the artist's rendition of light that shone through the liquids, bent and separated into the colors that made up the spectrum of God's covenantal rainbow. Then, E.V. added more droplets, complete with all seven colored lines like a miniature rainbow inside each drop. The beautiful and expressive mini rainbows flowed on the outer and brighter side of the window. The drops lightened in tone until they became as crystal clear rain water that cascaded past the glass window to whatever was below.

E.V. studied the fine marker pens. Most were like new, because she rarely used such bright hues in her artwork. She angled her head from side to side and admired the changes. There was a knock on her bedroom door, and E.V. set the paper aside.

"Come in, Grams." Ruby entered. E.V. noticed that her grandmother held out a book with two hands. She wondered whether the woman's arthritis was kicking up again.

Ruby walked over to E.V.'s bed and sat down. "Here, girl. It's G-pa's Bible. I believe the time has come for you to have it."

E.V. thanked her grandmother, who stood and exited the room. E.V. kissed the book, looked upward, and whispered, "Thank you, G-pa Bill." E.V. glanced at her new bracelet, then opened the Word of God and became immersed. She had turned to John 3, where the Bible's red-ribbon bookmark rested. She wondered if it signaled the last passage her grandfather had read, or maybe it had been his favorite. She didn't know. E.V. pored through amazing and familiar verses until she felt herself grow weary.

E.V. was on a beach. A boat was rowed up to the sand and men in robes, laughing and joking, sprang from the vessel. The craft must have been from an ancient time, E.V. reasoned, as she paid attention to its details. The men began to tether the boat and work on the shoreline.

It was him. He stood there, smiling. His hair was wavy. Strong shoulders supported muscular upper arms, silhouetted beneath the sleeves of his robe. His hand reached out to hers. "Evangeline, I have been waiting for you." The broad smile could not be contained by the beard or even the whole of the entire face. His essence was love and joy.

"Am, am I dead?" she stuttered,

"No, child, you are more alive than most. Would you like to walk with me?"

"Jesus? Jesus, it's really you!"

He nodded once with a smile, "Let's walk." They communicated while sitting under a palm tree in the salt-infused breeze. The temperature was neither overly warm nor excessively cool. "You have opened your heart, Evangeline. For this, I am well pleased. I would like you to go farther, reach others, unlock hearts, Daughter."

She spoke, "How, and why me? I fall short and am just beginning to learn, myself."

Jesus smiled even bigger, "That is the whole point, Daughter. Others will soon begin to listen to the youth who will have much to carry. The wake-up call is upon your generation."

Evangeline looked out at the water and then back to the Lord and Savior, "Yes, and I am going to need a lot of help."

Jesus became more serious, "Truly, truly, I say to you, unless one is born of water and the Spirit, he cannot enter the kingdom of God. That which is born of the flesh is flesh, and that which is born of the

Spirit is spirit. Do not marvel that I said to you, 'You must be born anew.'" (John 3:5-7)

"I just read that, before I fell asleep—or, came here," she hesitated. "Jesus, I was baptized."

"Oh, yes, I was there," his eyes sparkled. "You will know, Evangeline, when it is time to call upon Holy Spirit to infuse you, so that you may be born again of his spirit and fire. Many others of all age groups are in need of the same medicine to heal and to cure. Your strength comes from me. Others see that strength. Some might call it grit," the Son of Man smiled. Jesus stood and again, extended his hand outward. E.V. held on and rose to her feet. They hugged for a long time. She could feel his very real heart beating against hers or possibly within her own.

E.V.'s eyes opened, and she was on her bed, thrilled but at the same time, sad and disappointed. She yearned to be with Jesus once again. Her mind replayed the beautiful experience. She felt an immense freedom. E.V. also recognized that she had been pressed into service. Evangeline had said yes to him from her own heart, and she needed to follow through. It was crystal clear in her dream, or perhaps it had been a vision.

Where to begin, she wondered. Aloud, E.V. voiced, "Jesus, I need you to tell me, so I can do the work for you." Three words began to play over and over again in Evangeline's heart: time, talent, and treasure.

She thought about it and then stood up and flipped open the paper planner on her desk. Hmm, she definitely no longer had the time she used to, especially in the last semester of her senior year. She assessed her talent and was thankful that she was involved in the music ministry at church. Her love for art was being filled up during play production and at home. E.V. pondered, what treasure did she have? She worked three part-time jobs but barely earned enough money for gasoline. Grams agreed to cover E.V.'s car insurance until she graduated. She also acknowledged that a treasure didn't have to be a monetary fixture.

Then, E.V. knew. G-pa Bill's legacy was one of her treasures. She needed to preserve his memory in some way. She prayed to know more about her role. E.V. decided to bring it to the next prayer gathering at the flag. She planned to request a silent prayer intention without providing any details. God would know what everyone was praying for.

E.V. regularly attended the online business club during the school week in addition to the group's social gatherings outside of school. Although the games they played were competitive, the teens were eager to work together. Everyone recognized that they had been learning more as a team than as individuals or even pairs. It had again cycled back to E.V.'s turn to host game night.

E.V. liked how the group respected its members while they still had a great time together. Even their disagreements were entertaining. Millie was talented when it came to looking at the broad picture of a game challenge and breaking it down to the smallest components. Frederick was often called the detail man down to the minutiae. Callista enjoyed taking small pieces of the games and reconstructing them to devise whole concepts that could be seen or used in new ways. Elijah was the team member who often appeared not to be paying attention until he suddenly came up with the solution to the endgame. They called Pete, "Honest Abe," from the reputation of Abraham Lincoln's character and integrity. Pete would rather lose a game or learn that he was wrong, than cheat or pretend that he knew something he didn't. E.V. just considered herself blessed to be around so many awesome people even though she had no gaming background nor did she care to increase those skills.

Pete had convinced Ruby to eat with the group that had gathered in her home. She obliged and entertained them for over an hour by detailing and then answering questions about the space program. The young guests' eyes grew wide when Ruby explained some of the theories purported that the space agency planted Easter eggs on the moon, in museums, and upon actual crafts.

"Like real hidden Easter eggs?" Millie questioned with surprise.

Ruby clarified, "It's an expression, Millie. They could be fun clues or substantial and pertinent information meant for future generations."

E.V. was rather surprised that Grams had offered so many specifics. The woman's spirits were high, and she stayed focused and positive. Callista asked Ruby how E.V.'s grandpa had felt about his wife's involvement in the space program. E.V. cringed at the question, but Grams remained lively. While Ruby discussed the latter part of Bill's life, she spoke about how he volunteered at a Veteran's home for the aging.

"That's it!" E.V. whispered.

Pete asked, "What is?" The group was staring at E.V.

E.V.'s tone was subdued, as her mind lingered in the depths of introspection. "Oh, I had been praying about something, and the Lord just gave me an answer," E.V. smiled with a definitive nod.

Pete was enthusiastic, "Awesome listening, Evangeline!" No one else commented, but they remained attentive.

The young people were starting to savor game nights at the Gold house. Computer gaming systems were not available. They delighted in the strategies of board games, word challenges, and puzzles. At the end of each evening, everyone helped E.V. pack up and put away the boxes before they left.

Pete was the last guest to say goodbye and asked E.V. if he could take her to dinner and then the school play. They had worked so hard to build sets and prepare props. Both thought it would be fun to be in the audience. E.V. knew the night could be costly, so she offered to go Dutch. Pete assured her that he earned his wages by working for the church, cleaning, setting up, and breaking down for each service. She said, yes. As independent as E.V. was, she had to admit that it felt special being taken care of and doted upon.

E.V. made a decision that evening. She would visit the old-age home where her grandfather had volunteered. After everyone went home, she tried convincing her grandmother to go with her. E.V. noted how optimistic and cheerful Grams had been when she was in the company of the teens. Nevertheless, the older woman declined to join her.

At dinner, before the show, the following week, Pete shared with Evangeline how different she was from other girls. She asked, "Should I be offended?"

"Not at all," he said. "It's a compliment. I'm proud to be with you, Evangeline."

She smiled and wanted to discuss her Jesus visions with Pete. However, E.V. just didn't know how or where to start. She let Pete know that although her schedule was busy, as soon as it opened, she wanted to join a Bible study at his church to keep learning.

"That'd be great, Evangeline!"

The next Sunday morning church service was eye-opening, heart-wrenching, and healing, all at the same time. Pastor Dave began his sermon by titling it, "From Sorrow to Joy." He spoke about his own time spent with youth in Christian formation. He briefly provided a superficial overview of what had happened at the festival. As a result, the Christian Youth Club was no longer welcomed at the public-school venue.

Pete's dad went on to teach, by citing his own observations, how easy it had been to shut down Christians from fear of the virus. The squelching also affected higher education as well as the post-pandemic world. At the same time, he openly accepted blame for his students who went on the attack during the festival. He reminded the congregation that even the Israelites grew weary and impatient for Moses to return from Mount Sinai in the book of Exodus. They had a festival that grew in debauchery and then created a golden calf to worship. Moses returned with the stone tablets that contained the Ten Commandments written by God's very own finger. Moses destroyed the tablets in his anger. He knew that the people betrayed their trust in the Lord even after God used Moses to lead the chosen people out of Egypt's bondage.

Dave paused and continued, "I look at our country, today. I look at our congregation, today. I look at our young people, today. Yes, children are resilient, but too much bending will cause breakage. Our youth are the future, and the very youth of today are broken. They are at worst, hopeless. At best, they move about in a gloomy mist, shrouded by indecisiveness, sadness, distraction, and the unknown." The pastor glanced down and referred to his notes, "I love John 16:20! Jesus has promised, 'Truly, truly, I say to you, you will weep and lament, but the world will rejoice; you will be sorrowful, but your sorrow will turn into joy.' In the last line of Chapter 16, Jesus promises, 'In the world you have tribulation; but be of good cheer, I have overcome the world.'" Dave looked back up at the congregation, "People of God, it's time to arise! We will soon be at our Easter celebration! Wake up! Stand up! Know why we are here! The Lord has a plan. Embrace that plan and trust to know we each have a part in it. We were born for a time such as this! There are no coincidences with God. How you will fulfil your mission on this side of heaven is up to you. Do not throw away your salvation. Jesus suffered, died, and rose for each of us. I will break from our usual routine and ask the worship singers and musicians to come up and take their places. This is long overdue, so we will now have an altar call."

As the musicians assembled, Pastor Dave prayed over the entire room of people. He asked Holy Spirit to move through those gathered so that anyone who wished to commit or recommit their life to Jesus would answer the call. All were invited to come up to the front for personal prayer. The musicians played with an automaticity that flowed. They barely needed to communicate. Praise songs arose from the group with ease.

E.V. was on the keyboard that morning. She was intensely caught up in the Spirt. She watched the first dozen people come up, have hands laid upon their heads, and receive prayer. Some rested in the

Spirit. Ushers availed themselves to safely catch members of the flock who fell back and then gently guide them to the floor. At times, Pastor Dave had to step aside to receive more people, taking care not to step on or bump into those who were having profound experiences. Some people stood, received their anointing, and returned to their places with tears, laughter, or a new sense of purpose.

E.V. felt the tug. At first, she resisted. Evangeline could not remember the exact moment she moved away from the keyboard and walked around to the front of the altar and stood before Jesus. Of course, Evangeline was well aware that she was facing Pastor Dave. However, when she closed her eyes, she saw Jesus, the same Jesus she spent time with in her dream or vision on the beach.

The church leader greeted the young woman, "Welcome, Evangeline. Do you repent of your sins?"

"Yes," E.V. emphatically stated.

"Evangeline, Jesus Christ suffered and died for us. Do you fully accept him into your heart as your Lord and Savior?"

"I do," E.V. declared. She suddenly had that same sensation of Jesus' beating heart, rhythmically synchronized within her own.

When Pastor Dave laid his hands upon Evangeline's head, he had a word of knowledge for her. "Abba is well-pleased with your progress, Daughter. There is more, much more." E.V. nodded. "Then be born again, and follow him," Pastor Dave professed.

Evangeline only remembered being aided to her feet by Tammy and Wayne before she made her way back to the worship band. However, E.V. had clearly heard what she interpreted as her mom's voice just before she stood up, "Continue to know my story, Evangeline. I too, need a legacy." It seemed to E.V. like she had been gone from the music group for a long time. When she returned to the keyboard, the band was still playing the same song as when she stepped away.

CHAPTER THIRTEEN

REPLAY

On the first Monday of Spring Break, E.V. slept in. She certainly had plans to wake up early, but her body decided otherwise when she hit the dismiss button on her phone alarm. Shortly after 10 a.m., she was roused by her phone vibrating. She tried to sound as awake as possible but answered with a groggy, "Hello?"

"Hey, Evangeline." After a pause, "It's me, Pete. Did I wake you?"

"Well, that depends what time it is," her voice faltered. She yawned and rubbed her eyes. When E.V. tried to sit up, she flopped back down on the bed.

"Okay, you go back to sleep. I'll talk with you later," he decided.

They both said goodbye. E.V. shut her eyes, but they popped open and she shot straight up in bed. Her breath quickened. She attempted to focus on something that was not in the room. She immediately hit redial for Pete's number. He answered right away. "Don't go," she stated.

"Don't go where?" he questioned.

She raised her voice, "Don't go to the springs!"

Pete grew serious. "Evangeline, what's going on?"

"Where are you?" she pressed.

"I'm in my parents' van at a gas station just off the highway. The family ran into a convenience store, so I thought I'd call to say hi. We're on our way into the city to pick up supplies for the church. On the way back, we're stopping at the springs I had invited you to, so we can have a picnic."

The teen sounded desperate. "Please, Pete, put me on speaker phone when your parents are back in the car." Evangeline heard car doors, voices, and shuffling sounds. Pete announced that Evangeline was on the line and wanted to say something.

"Okay, we can all hear you, Evangeline," Pete sounded uncertain.

"This is E.V., uh, Evangeline."

Pete's dad spoke and then listened. "Good morning, Evangeline. How can we help you?"

"Please don't go to the springs, Pastor."

Pastor Dave remained calm, "May I ask why not?"

Evangeline stammered, "I, I do not know, exactly."

There was a moment of silence from the Marshall phone line. Janet began, "Let's all pray about it, together."

They took turns and asked for the Lord's protection, wisdom, and guidance. Pete's older sister was not in the vehicle, but both of his younger brothers were. E.V. was last to pray, and the two youngest passengers shouted, "Amen!" The parents quietly chuckled and thanked the younger boys for their enthusiasm. Pete and his parents grew serious.

Janet chimed in, "Evangeline is right, Dave. I can sense something."

Pete interjected, "I stand in agreement."

"Wait," E.V. wedged in a thought. "Let's test and discern the spirit of what's happening in the name of Jesus Christ, the one true God." They all prayed and waited.

Dave said that although he did not discern any warning, he would change plans after securing the church supplies. Three confirmations were more than enough for the reverend. The family continued on their way. Pete took E.V. off speaker phone and quietly thanked her for listening and sharing what she had heard. He promised to call when they were driving home.

E.V. dragged herself out of bed and into the bathroom. She washed her face and pulled on a clean outfit. After her hair was brushed and tied back into a ponytail, E.V. headed to the kitchen. She greeted her grandmother and without hesitation, jumped into what had transpired.

Ruby listened and then asked, "Was it a knowing, Eves?"

"I'm pretty sure it was, Grams," she replied with a nod. "It was so strong. It still is." The teen poured herself a bowl of cereal and sat at the table. "I hope I saw it wrong. It was something major."

Ruby bowed her head. "I pray for anyone involved and that the Marshalls will be safe."

"Amen," affirmed Evangeline. "Grams, I'm going to the veteran's home where G-pa Bill used to visit. Want to come?"

"No thanks, child, but how nice! May I ask what sparked that idea?"

"Not what, but who?" E.V. laughed. "Grams, I was motivated that night when you shared some of your and G-pa's amazing life experiences with my friends. I want amazing life experiences, too!"

In under an hour, E.V had arrived and introduced herself to the receptionist at Eastern Florida Lakes Veterans Home. She enquired as to whom she could speak with. E.V. was ushered into a small office. Less than fifteen minutes later, she was escorted through a hallway and introduced to a nurse who suggested that E.V. make herself available to the residents as a visitor.

The teen was surprised by how conversations melded with ease. Some residents were quite sharp. Many had obvious memory impairments as well as physical infirmities. A number of the men wore hats that depicted in which war and branch of the military they had served. E.V. met many people in that living room during her one-hour visit. She got them books and magazines from a rack. E.V. helped one woman string beads to make a necklace. An elderly man asked if E.V. would refill his cup with ice water from a cooler on the other side of the room. It didn't take her long to recognize that staff numbers were limited.

When E.V. arrived home that afternoon, she was looking forward to sharing her positive experience with Grams. Instead, her grandmother asked if she had heard about the multi-car pileup. E.V. asked if it was anywhere near the springs where the Marshalls had been planning to spend the afternoon. "Yes, as a matter of fact, it was just before that exit in the eastbound lanes."

Soon after, Pete called to enquire whether his family might stop by on their way home. E.V. checked with Grams, who approved. "I'll make some coffee," Grams offered. She stood and walked to the kitchen. Ruby only used her cane when outside their home. However, for the first time, E.V. noticed some similarities in her grandmother's gait when compared to the older folks at the Veterans home. It made the granddaughter uncomfortable.

The doorbell rang. E.V. raised her voice, "I'll get it!" She expected Pete to be standing at the door. However, it was Pastor Dave.

Ruby came to the front inner hallway. "Please invite them all in, girl." Grams led the way to the living room, but when Pete's younger brothers saw the plate of cookies, it was clear to Janet that it might be best if they met in the kitchen. Once cookies, milk, and coffee were set out, the conversation veered to E.V.'s knowings.

Pete's father began, "Evangeline, I would like to address this in the presence of your grandmother, Mrs. Gold, if I may."

"Please, call me Ruby, and is E.V. in some sort of trouble, Reverend?" E.V. waited near the table. The uneven stance and fidgeting of her hands made it clear to Ruby that her granddaughter felt unsure.

"Oh, my apologies, ladies," Pastor Dave began. "Peter and Evangeline, please sit with the rest of us." The two teens pulled up stools from the center island counter. They sat next to one another and joined the group at the large colonial-style circular table. Dave continued, "Evangeline, are you prophetic?"

"I'm not really sure, Pastor Dave. I've had dreams and feelings since I was little."

Janet added, "We did not go to the springs on our way home but saw two air-evac helicopters taking off over the trees not far from there. The electronic highway signs alerted all that the other road was closed and to take alternate routes." E.V. nodded.

Pete filled in the storyline, "I checked on social media. There was a head-on collision that caused a vehicle rollover. Another crossed the median and impacted more cars. It sounded like a disaster with cars and trucks slamming into one another. Had we not changed plans and stopped to eat lunch in our van after loading up the church supplies, we might have been at the scene around the time it all happened."

E.V.'s slightly raised eyebrows said more than her exhaled, "Oh." Pete placed a supportive arm on her shoulder for a moment.

They all prayed for those involved and thanked their Father in heaven for his guidance and protection. God was praised for E.V. knowing to call and warn the family. Everyone declared an amen. The younger boys immediately returned to the cookies and milk at hand.

Spring break, E.V. noted, progressed quickly as school vacations usually did. The next day, she and Pete went to a local park after work. Since they were together that afternoon, they also attended a Bible study the same night. Tammy and Wayne Connor offered a continuing series one evening each week. That night's teaching was based on Ephesians 4:11 and the influence of apostles, prophets, evangelists, pastors, and teachers. After the focus on the five-fold ministry, Evangeline approached the pastor once the service had ended. "Pastor Dave, I have prayed and do not believe that I'm a prophet."

He offered with sincerity, "Maybe not, Evangeline, but you are prophetic. Keep praying and discerning. The Lord will let you know." Just then, Tammy and Wayne Connor walked over and said goodbye for the evening. They mentioned that they had much planned during their time off from school. The couple wished Dave and his family a blessed remainder of the week. The church leader waited a moment and then called them back. The Connors turned around. "This just came to me. Tammy, would you be willing to mentor Evangeline? She is learning rapidly and has many gifts of the Spirit."

With warmth and understanding, Mrs. Connor smiled at E.V. before she looked toward Dave. "I'll pray about it, Pastor."

That interchange was the impetus Evangeline needed to acknowledge that sometimes, one did not understand God's will without asking him to reveal it. Pastor Dave agreed that Tammy should pray and discern whether she was to stand as a coach to E.V. at that time.

E.V. made a decision to listen within her heart. She remained decidedly open to whatever the Lord had for her. She wondered whether Pastor Dave purposely asked Mrs. Connor publicly, and in front of E.V., instead of privately. Perhaps, she pondered, it was to drive home the importance of prayer as well as trust in discernment.

That evening in her bedroom, E.V. opened Bonnie's diary for the first time in weeks. She was able to see her mother in a new light. Bonnie was fun and loved to have fun. E.V. caught herself giggling aloud while reading about some of the antics Bonnie and her friends had been involved in. E.V. admired how loyal and compassionate a friend Bonnie had been. When the grandmother of Lily, Bonnie's friend, passed away, E.V. felt the pain projected through her mother's voice and captured in the writing. According to E.V.'s maternal scribe, Bonnie not only created a handmade card, but attended the funeral, and spent extra time with Lily. The grieving young friend was frequently invited to spend the weekend at the Gold's house, where there would be times of reflection as well as laughter. Bonnie appeared to be such a supportive friend that E.V. paused to wonder why her mother might not have received similar encouragement and comfort from her own inner circle. But then again, maybe she had.

Just reading about the death of a beloved grandparent caused E.V. to wince and close the book on that segment of Bonnie Gold's life. The pain of losing G-pa Bill was raw, once again. E.V. knew that her wound had not been completely healed, but it had at least scabbed over. The scab had again been peeled away from E.V.'s heart, and the gash began to ooze.

It had been a long time since E.V. cried herself to sleep. That night, E.V. also cried out with praise and blessings to God. A third chain evaporated as light increased. Evangeline opened her eyes and was at first, disoriented. The nightstand light was still on. The diary rested next to her on the bed. She repositioned herself, placed the book back on the bedside table, and switched off the light. E.V. shut her eyes but then quickly reopened them in the dark. She had definitely dreamed another scene.

The sounds of her cries were replayed, but it was praise for the Lord in song. She felt as if she might have been talking or singing in her sleep. It was so real. She whispered out loud, "Praise you, Almighty and Living Lord. I love you. I want what you want for me."

When E.V. opened her eyes again, it was morning. She checked her phone and since there were no dog-walking or baby-sitting assignments on her schedule, E.V. decided to return to the Veterans home. Once again, she invited her grandmother, who declined because of an appointment with Dr. Davis and another with an eye doctor.

On that second visit, the director of nursing told E.V. that the people living in the memory care wing had very few visitors. E.V. agreed to enter the hallway but initially, experienced an eerie feeling when the doors were locked behind her. She introduced herself to Vicky, the nurse in charge of the wing. Vicky assured E.V. that she only had to ask a staff member to unlock the combination code when she was ready to leave. Vicky explained that those residents might wander off, so the locked unit was for their own safety. E.V. immediately thought of her dreams where chains held her to the stone walls. She looked around the warm, homelike hallway, the over-sized large, bright den, and was then able to dispel the uncomfortable notions.

E.V. met some of the assistant nurses, cleaning crew, and food services personnel. She was impressed with how politely they treated the residents. E.V. stepped outside where there was a bright, fenced-in patio with shaded areas. Elderly people walked about and sat in wheelchairs and upon benches. There was a nice-looking man who seemed too young to live there. His name was Robert. E.V. engaged him in conversation, and he told her that he had been special ops in the military. E.V. thanked him for his service. A husband-and-wife team who also lived on that floor were enjoying the outdoor area. She had been an army nurse and he claimed to have been a fighter pilot, although E.V. was unsure. Nevertheless, they were a single-minded team. He remembered what she did not, and she helped her husband with what he could no longer do by himself. A friendly lady, named Lavender, began telling E.V. stories about her time training as a shuttle mission astronaut. She had colorful stories and even more colorful language, which made E.V. laugh.

During supper, E.V. shared her excitement in meeting so many fine people at the senior home. "Grams," she began slowly and moved the mashed potatoes around on her plate at the same pace. She then looked up at her grandmother, "I met a woman there, who said she was an astronaut and spoke about the shuttle program."

"Really?" Grams asked with composure. "What was her name?"

E.V. replied, "It was Lavender."

Ruby lowered her fork, "Lavender Foley?"

"I didn't get her full name, Grams."

Chapter Fourteen

BREAKTHROUGH

Ruby readily recalled the name of the woman she trained with. Lavender did not fly on the missions but was hired for her computer skills. Ruby was at first hesitant but then decided to take E.V. up on her offer to pay Miss Lavender a visit. Upon meeting, Lavender Foley did not remember Ruby Gold, but the latter surely remembered the woman as a cohort from their program preparation. The three sat outdoors on the shaded patio. As Lavender spoke, Ruby and E.V. both listened to details that exuded a rich clarity.

Lavender remarked about the government's involvement to make the Mission 25 disaster look like an accident. Ruby had heard numerous conspiracy theories over the years but never expected it to come from the mouth of someone she considered, a demented old lady. Nonetheless, the discussions were quite real to Ruby. Lavender and Ruby hit it off right away. Lavender asked both Ruby and E.V. to please return again for a visit. After they all said goodbye, Ruby quietly pulled a nurse to the side and asked, "Is Lavender, you know, with it?"

The nurse responded with a shake of the head, "Only when she believes she's working at mission control or teaching about one of the orbiter's computer systems."

Ruby needed to hold the wall railings as she made her way down the hall and out to the parking lot. E.V. had gone ahead to start the car and air conditioner, so it would be cool for her grandmother. The ride home was quiet. E.V. attempted to break the silence with conversation. She let Grams know the gaming group would gather that evening, and E.V. would drive to the location. Ruby's response was simply, "Okay, dear."

During that next gaming session, the teens met at the Connor home. They had the best internet speed, so the young people hoped the gaming project might prove to become more fun at Elijah's house. The friends had begun to play an online merchandising team game. They decided on the commerce division to explore whether they could all collaborate on a simulation to detect how well they'd work together in a business venture.

"Why wait for graduation?" Frederick had tossed out at the start of the project.

When the game was initially too complex for E.V., she declared it a cockamamie plan. The other youth were thoroughly amused, and Evangeline had to explain that it was a word she grew up hearing from her grandparents.

Millie added, "Cockamamie ideas can lead to creative inventions."

E.V. wasn't convinced that the game could actually amount to real business prospects, but she enjoyed spending time with her peers. Frederick and Callista had been grumbling that even at Elijah's house, the game continued to lag just like it had done the week before at Callista's home. That was when the two suggested they shut it down and pursue a board game.

"Let me get my dad," Elijah offered. "He probably doesn't know the game, but he's the most experienced computer guy here." The others nodded and ate popcorn while Elijah left the room.

Wayne Connor entered the area and greeted, "Hey everyone, how may I assist?" Elijah followed his father. The man agreed that the electronic game was unknown to him but asked his son to demonstrate what was going on. Elijah walked his father through the system. The students revealed similar perceptions of how the artificial intelligence of background characters appeared overly prominent, and their locations became inconsistent. Non-player characters became ill-timed with the scene movements just prior to delays, and then the game would shut itself down.

The high school computer instructor repeatedly tried various actions and key strokes. He finally declared, "There may be a bug in the code or within the game loop. The graphics in these games appear faster than the eye can register, so we might not notice picture variations during a particular moment of the sequence." Elijah and Frederick nodded. The others paid close attention. E.V. furrowed her brow. "When all else fails," Mr. Connor continued, pressed the power button, and unplugged the device, "try a hard shutdown. I hope you all don't mind." The maneuver evoked a few grimaces. "Where'd you get this game from, anyway, son?"

Elijah barely looked up, "It was a freebie from a drug company. They were giving away samples in our health class. It was packaged like an old-fashioned disc, but once you opened it, there was a code for the digital download."

Wayne gave his wife a funny look as she entered the room. E.V. searched the Connors' expressions. Tammy had just brought out more drinks and began asking what the students were doing the next day for Easter. She invited all the teens and their families to the sunrise service on a nearby local beach. Faces lit up at the word, beach. There was a discussion about how early they'd need to arrive. That was when the excitement plummeted. After all, teenagers were rarely known to be early risers. "E.V., I'd imagine that Pete couldn't make it here tonight with the Marshalls working to get everything prepared for morning." E.V. nodded to acknowledge Mrs. Connor's comment.

After Elijah turned the computer system back on, they waited for the game to reboot. That took the group back to the program's startup. Most didn't mind after all, since they quickly remembered what did and didn't work in previous attempts. Together, they strategized alternative routes to level up. Frederick argued that he didn't recall the initial configuration of the video game looking the same way it had just presented. Finally, the group decided to call it an early evening.

On a peaceful Florida beach before dawn the next morning, E.V. found herself at the inspiring church service titled, "A Resurrection Celebration at Sunrise." Afterwards, she drove back in the direction of her house. E.V. had sent a message to Grams to enquire whether she would like to come back to the beach for Sunday brunch. While she awaited the response, E.V. debated about whether she should stop at a store to buy some treats for the church picnic in addition to those in her wing of the Veterans home. She began to refer to the memory care unit as her home wing. For a reason that made no cognitive sense to E.V., she diverted the car from a local road and merged onto the highway. She turned at the second exit, Coastal Drive. The young woman found herself in the nursing home parking lot, shaking her head back and forth. A smile crept through and parted the corners of her mouth.

Ruby messaged E.V. back with, "No, thank you. Enjoy yourself." After the initial visit with Lavender and Ruby, E.V. noticed that her grandmother was withdrawn and downcast. Grams didn't want to get up early for the Easter sunrise service at the beach and said she'd probably go to their old standby church. Thus, E.V. had attended the shoreline gathering without Ruby. Since Pete was occupied with helping his family after the service, E.V. told him she'd be back soon. Her original plan was to pick up Grams and return.

Eastern Florida Lakes Veterans Home boldly beckoned E.V. She parked, walked through the front sliding glass doors, and approached the mechanical interface. The familiar electronic tablet used to register guests, sported a new announcement bar that scrolled along the top edge. It warned that numerous residents were ill, and if visitors had any symptoms from a list that dropped down from the menu, they were encouraged not to enter. An additional paper sign had been taped to both inner glass doors that read, "Attention: masks recommended."

E.V. noticed the paper, but she focused on the clock that recorded the check-in time. She assured herself that there was already plenty of food in the cooler inside her car for the brunch back at the beach. That encouraged E.V. that there was no need to shop further, so there'd be time for a quick visit to her home wing. E.V. peered through the central glass patio doors and could see many children scurrying about the inner lawn. The staff had advertised an Easter egg hunt. Chairs lined the sidewalk for the residents and visiting family members.

An attendant recognized E.V. and asked whether the teen wanted to enter the memory care wing. It struck E.V. as ironic because the doors remained locked on Resurrection Day. She nodded with lips pressed together. Her mind shifted back to the pandemic and how nursing homes had been kept shuttered on lockdown. She endured an image of her new elderly friends being enclosed inside their own Easter eggs, hidden away from the world to be seen only by some. E.V. had learned that most residents would spend an average of three years at the home before passing on to whatever waited for them in the next world. Easter eggs often represented the tomb that could not contain Christ.

"Just maybe!" she exclaimed aloud and then looked around to check whether anyone had noticed that she was talking to herself. She contemplated that maybe, just maybe, her friends had stumbled upon an Easter egg of sorts in the gaming program. What if it wasn't a programming glitch at all? What if it was a blueprint intended to be recognized by very few and discarded by most? Both her grandparents often explained that hints were often meant to be obscured by the obvious that stood in plain view. Maybe, whoever cracked the code would get a prize, she mused.

E.V. heard her name and turned sharply. She quickly wondered if it was because she was mumbling out loud or wasn't wearing a mask. The woman introduced herself as Linda, the activities director of Eastern Florida Lakes Veterans Home. Linda shared that she was glad to have caught up with E.V., although she hadn't expected her to volunteer on Easter Sunday. Linda asked if she could have a word with her.

The director of activities said she noticed how much time and talent E.V. invested with the residents. She had watched her help them color, paint, and work on jewelry-making projects. Linda was sure that E.V. was a talented artist. She mentioned that she was there on the holiday because the weekend activities worker had resigned. Linda asked if E.V. would be interested in a part-time weekend position. She asked Evangeline why she became a volunteer at the home. E.V. reminisced about how her grandfather, Bill Gold, used to visit the Veterans facility for the service people who had become physically or mentally disabled. Sometimes, her grandfather would explain, the residents suffered from both types of afflictions. She mentioned how Bill used to express that he was blessed to serve his country and his God. E.V. shared that her visits there were a way to honor his memory and honor those who had also served their country.

Linda added, "E.V., you've carried on your grandfather's legacy. Your parents must be very proud of you."

E.V. returned, "My grandparents are the only parents I've ever known. And yes, I'd be very interested in a weekend job, thank you." They both exchanged information and agreed to meet that next week.

Evangeline moved to the outdoor area. The grounds were well kept and the smell of fresh-cut grass was interwoven with memories of a carefree childhood and summer. Of course, grass grew all year in Florida, yet E.V. always said the trimming of summer grass was attached to its own fond memories and sweet new growth. She felt somewhat detached as children scrambled for treats and families visited with loved ones. E.V. wished a few of the folks a happy Resurrection Day. She promised to return the following weekend. E.V. was more than surprised when Lavender wheeled herself close by and boldly verbalized, "Go home and see your grandmother, young lady." E.V. nodded and thanked her.

The beach gathering provided a fresh view for Evangeline, who had never been to an outdoor church service. She could not keep from being reminded about her vision of Jesus and his Apostles, where she had spent personal time with the Lord on a beautiful beach. After brunch, E.V. helped the church members clean and pack up the tables and equipment. Pete came over and shared that his mom had invited Evangeline for Easter dinner at their home. She thanked him profusely, but told Pete that she decided to go home to spend time with Ruby. She reasoned that she hadn't yet seen her grandmother that day. Pete assured her that Ruby would also be welcomed at their house. E.V. smiled and said that she'd let him know if plans changed. She also asked Pete to thank his mom for the kind offer. As he walked E.V. to her car, they held hands. Before she entered her vehicle, they kissed. E.V. got into her car feeling very grateful for the special people that God had brought into her life. How different her life had become since laying it down before the Lord. She waved goodbye, put on the seatbelt, and settled into the driver's seat of Mimi. Her whole life, not just the vehicle, had become as comfortable as an old pair of jeans.

E.V. pulled forward in her driveway. When she opened the kitchen door, she expected to smell the aromas of a holiday meal. However, there was nothing of the sort, not even tea brewing. E.V. set everything on the kitchen table and made her way into the house. She was not sure what she would find. The second car was in the driveway, so her grandmother was home.

"Grams?" E.V. gently called, as she made her way through the quiet house.

Her grandmother was in the sewing room, which at one time, was Bonnie's bedroom. When E.V. stepped inside, Ruby spoke, "Oh, hello child, I didn't hear your car."

Again, the teen repeated the address, "Grams?"

"Yes, dear."

"Are you okay?"

The elderly woman patted the loveseat. E.V. sat down next to her. Ruby had been going through old pictures. Bill and Ruby's wedding album was left opened and set aside on a small table. "Look at this, Eves. This album had Bonnie and Bradley's school pictures from kindergarten on up through high school graduations. Soon, I'll add your graduation pictures to these pages."

"Grams, I'm not anywhere else in that book. Have you eaten yet, today?"

"Of course, child," Ruby laughed. "We had stew."

"That was last night, Grams. Did you go to church?"

"Oh, no, was that today, E.V.?"

"Yes, Grams. Let's go into the kitchen and have something to eat." E.V. helped her grandmother up. There were no dishes in the sink or drainboard. E.V. put on water for tea and made her grandmother a sandwich. E.V. waited for Ruby to eat. The light came back into the older woman's eyes. They spoke little. E.V. wanted to drive her grandmother to the emergency room after the woman had consumed some nourishment. Ruby refused and insisted she was fine.

E.V. remained concerned. She stayed with her grandmother until she was certain that the episode may have been caused by loneliness, dehydration, and a lack of food. E.V. made a decision that she would spend more time with Grams. "Guess who I saw at the Veterans home, today?"

"Who?" Grams questioned.

"Lavender Foley," E.V. answered lightly.

Her grandmother's face dropped, "Oh."

"Grams, she told me to go home and spend time with you. Here I am."

"That's nice, Eves."

"Grams, I think you should see Dr. Davis, soon. If you want me to go with you, I can take a few hours off from school."

Ruby nodded, "You're right, child, and I'm fine to drive myself, thank you."

Evangeline became animated, "Why don't we put in a movie to watch? I can make popcorn," she smiled.

"That sounds nice, Eves," Ruby agreed.

E.V. allowed Grams to walk by herself into the living room but stayed nearby to watch Ruby's movements. Her grandmother certainly seemed to have regained her usual strength. E.V. brought her another cup of brewed tea and said she'd start some popcorn and return shortly. Grams sat on the sofa and put on the TV with a remote while she waited for E.V. When the teen returned, her grandmother was watching a news bulletin claiming word of a new virus from overseas. The two anchors took turns reassuring their audience.

"Please, don't panic," the anchorwoman with perfect hair and makeup spewed.

Her co-anchor broadcast, "This time, we've be assured, they'll be ready with an attenuated vaccine that can be administered in a variety of modalities." His bright, artificially-applied smile reminded E.V. of a caricature in a political meme.

"Let's turn this junk off," insisted E.V. She put on an old comedy movie that Grams and Bill used to watch. For the first time, E.V. understood all the innuendos and thought it was very funny. Ruby seemed far away and politely laughed every time E.V. did.

Later that evening, E.V. made some pancakes, eggs, and sausages. "Happy Easter, Grams! Sorry I was out for so long, today, but now we can enjoy our Easter breakfast together," she smiled.

Grams chuckled, "Oh girl, I sure do love you. Happy Easter, Bonnie!"

"Promise me, Grams, tomorrow, you will make an appointment to see Dr. Davis."

"I promise, girl."

Chapter Fifteen
TRIALS

In Evangeline's opinion, Ruby was in free fall and about to enter a nosedive in both, her emotional and cognitive states. E.V. also began to note difficulties in her grandmother's physical ability to ambulate. Grams later checked her calendar and realized she had already scheduled an appointment with Dr. Davis. When E.V. got home from school, she enquired about the meeting and then specifically asked whether Grams had brought up the visit with Miss Lavender Foley.

Ruby relayed that her therapist thought it had been a good idea for the two women to meet. Dr. Davis asked whether it helped Ruby to see that life went on for others in the space program. Ruby apparently countered that it didn't do any good for Lavender, since she ended up in a locked memory care unit of a nursing home for the rest of her life sentence. The teen sighed at Ruby's own reality check. She also enquired how her grandmother's recent eye doctor appointment had gone. Grams said it was, "Okay," and offered no further information. Ruby did add that Dr. Davis thought it might be wise for her to make an appointment with her internist, and E.V. couldn't have agreed more.

The weekend brought orientation and training for E.V.'s new job position. She even fit in a visit with her home wing. The duties included providing activities in the main living room of Eastern Florida Lakes in addition to her beloved wing. There were crafts to be created as well as games to be set up and played. E.V. couldn't believe they were going to pay her to have fun. When Evangeline greeted Lavender Foley, the woman didn't recognize her.

E.V. quickly learned that employees often behaved differently when they were around coworkers versus the public. She still appreciated the services provided to the nursing home residents, but E.V. noticed subtle differences shortly after she became an employee. For example, a woman in food prep commented to one in the janitorial division that her ex had been served a restraining order. Vicky, the nurse in memory care, spoke with a young, wide-eyed nursing assistant about doing the right thing in getting rid of the blob. But there were also those with wisdom who spoke little and worked hard for the patients. E.V. took it all in.

That night, the online business gaming group met at her home. After dinner, Elijah shared something new. He brought a laptop and another device. Frederick recognized the portable Wi-Fi hotspot but asked about the laptop. Elijah said it was a local server that he had constructed on a spare laptop. "It could help us game here, tonight. I've loaded everything onto this server," he patted the laptop.

E.V. asked lots of questions. Pete had heard of both components but had never used either. Millie and Callista had little hands-on experience and varied amounts of knowledge.

"You built something inside your laptop?" E.V. questioned in amazement.

Elijah nodded in the affirmative. "My dad and I worked on it. It was fun!"

Then, Elijah and Frederick set up the connections, and the game began. They decided to choose different characters and then worked past the startup. The teens each took turns recommending how to proceed based on their last gaming efforts. They began to play and quickly recaptured the initial levels. Once again, the program quit.

Millie voiced, "I believe that since this was a free trial, and no offense to you, Elijah, the game's creator decided clients could only go this far before having to purchase the real thing. Video games are supposed to keep us excited and involved. I'm bored. Let's play one of E.V.'s cool board games."

E.V. slowly added, "Maybe," drawing out the two syllables.

Pete posed his question with a quizzical expression, "Maybe, meaning perhaps play a board game, or maybe we've reached the end of this video game?" E.V. was quiet. "Come on, Evangeline," he coaxed with a small sideways smile, "I know that silence."

She also smiled but with satisfaction that Pete really was getting to know her. E.V. did not often allow such closeness. "Just a hunch," she quipped, "but what if the gaming company hid an Easter egg in the program, you know, like a clue for a prize or to get to the next level?"

The rest responded to E.V.'s epiphany with questioning facial expressions. The group was nearly silent. E.V. scanned each person. Most glanced around the space and fixed their eyes in various positions of introspection. Callista rolled a key fob in her hand. Millie tapped her feet. Elijah had one ankle crossed over his opposite knee and played with a lace that dangled from one of his basketball shoes. Frederick rubbed his chin. They all decided they were done for the night.

E.V. had a follow-up appointment after school the next day with Dr. Davis. She got home very late the night before and was exhausted. She considered rescheduling but wanted to talk about her concerns for Ruby, which was exactly how the teenager opened up their scheduled time together.

Dr. Davis assured E.V. that her grandmother had recently been in for a visit. E.V. acknowledged but wanted to share that she had observed some challenging changes. Dr. Davis said she wanted to know how Evangeline was doing, and perhaps the three of them could meet together at another time, so there'd be no breach of privacy issues. E.V. acquiesced.

Dr. Davis referred back to imagery cards from E.V.'s initial evaluation that the teen had left unanswered. The first card depicted two dogs running in a park. Dr. Davis pointed to the card and asked E.V. which dog was ahead. The teen smiled, "A dog with or without a head is still a dog. Or is it?"

Dr. Davis went on, "What can you tell me about the unseen in the picture, Evangeline?"

"Well, I was never one of those people who could easily believe what I couldn't see. Belief based just on feelings would be the same as weighing an empty basket to check what it contains. However, now that I've given my life to Christ, I can believe."

"I do understand that, Evangeline. Could you provide an example of how that applied to your past?" Dr. Davis asked.

"Sure. I couldn't see my own earthly mother or father. Therefore, I was incapable of believing in them."

"How about now, Evangeline?"

The girl easily replied, "They did in fact exist, yet to me, my parents will always be Ruby and Bill Gold. Is that wrong, Doc?"

"No, not at all. It's a healthy way to separate out what's important for your life, Evangeline. From what you've shared, you and the young man, Pete, appear to have a good relationship." E.V. did not respond, but she was listening. "Do you believe in love, Evangeline?"

E.V. sighed, "I guess, for some."

"Evangeline, Are you able to see love with your eyes, or touch it with a stick?"

"No."

"Yet, it exists," Dr. Davis assured her.

"Like I said," E.V. fixed her eyes on the woman and firmly set her own shoulders, "for some."

Dr. Davis responded, "You have grit, Evangeline."

"So, I've been told," E.V. nodded. The teenager looked to one side and then upward until her eyes squared off with the doctor's. "Grit can make one," she breathed, "gritty."

"Good analysis, Evangeline," Dr. Davis smiled. "You may have a future in my line of work. Let me know if you'd ever be interested in job shadowing. Evangeline, would you like to meet again after today's appointment?"

"The chickens will still be there, tomorrow. What difference will one more or less egg make in the grand scheme of things?"

The woman chuckled, "Evangeline, come back anytime; but for now, I see no reason to schedule any further appointments for you. It's been refreshing to meet with you."

As final exams were approaching, Millie, Callista, and E.V. spoke about getting together to work on a school project. They were in the same math course that met during different periods of the day, so they approached the teacher. The instructor thought it was a novel idea and gave them permission to hypothetically rebuild the partial computer game utilizing a schematic diagram with an included discussion. The students agreed to collaborate at Callie's house.

After noting the same software snag while procrastinating on the development of their school project, Callista attempted to recreate small parts of the game and then discovered that the glitch was not a glitch at all. The software had been blocked to prevent further movement without a specific program key to unlock it. The girls needed to explain each step to E.V., as she was not as tech savvy as the rest. The school project did not require them to reveal the final solution of the game but rather to troubleshoot the problem and propose how the system could be rebuilt. They called Elijah and asked him to bring his server over. Since it contained a copy of the game, it could theoretically be used to create a template for what they needed in order to proceed. He didn't live far and said he'd be there soon.

They puzzled out particulars into the late hours of the night and were eventually joined by Pete and Frederick. Many computers were running. All brainpower was engaged. As the majority worked through computations, formulas, and multiple copies of the sequence itself, E.V. plugged in numbers on an older model PC. "Hey, guys, this is kind of cool," she noted. The teens continued with what E.V. termed their incessant, "mumbling, fumbling, and grumbling."

She was pretty sure they were just letting her play on a desktop. "Really, you should come see this." Pete walked over and joined her. He viewed the screen over E.V.'s shoulder. She looked up and flashed him a big smile. "Watch, I'll plug in any number, large or small. I think there's a pattern going on, here." Pete paid attention.

"Hey, Elijah," Pete called and motioned with his head to the screen that he and E.V. studied.

Elijah joined them and asked without taking his eyes off the monitor, "What'd you enter, E.V.?"

She shrugged, "Just some random stuff that I copied from a small line of copyright."

Simultaneously, Pete and Elijah repeated, "Copyright?"

Elijah pursued, "E.V., please show us that copyright."

"Well," she began, "I don't exactly remember how to get back to that point." The boys sighed. "But I thought it would make a cool art design that I could customize, so I reproduced it here." She opened her notebook and pointed to the line.

Elijah's eyes grew wide as saucers as he exclaimed, "Mind blowing! That's no copyright, E.V. It's code!"

"And hidden in plain view, just like an Easter egg," she laughed.

On Friday evening, Ruby agreed to join E.V. and Pete at a healing service at Pastor Dave's church. Ruby had been personally invited by the Marshalls days before and did not feel it would be proper to back out, even though she was tired. Dave had summoned other pastors from local churches as well as from distances. They covered a number of denominations and affiliations. All believed in the one, true God. There were rumors of another lockdown, so there was a sense that a healing service was needed for individuals, the church, and the country.

Ruby had continued in a downward spiral of memory, affect, and physical pain. E.V. stayed by her side the entire night and decided not to take part in playing the music. She prayed that God might touch her precious grandmother who had given so much of herself.

After Scripture readings, a sermon, and group prayers to decree and declare, the assembly was invited forward. Worship music permeated every space. Ruby slowly made her way to the front of the church. Evangeline supported her grandmother's free arm. The other one leaned upon the cane. When she approached a pastor who she had never met, Ruby began to repent quietly but aloud. In her emotional catharsis, Ruby listed her lackadaisical child-rearing modes, shame for by not being on the Challenger Space Shuttle, and other shortcomings, which included paying for the abortion. Once Ruby confessed to the Lord, she received great reconciliation while she was prayed over and anointed with oil by the man of God at the front of her line. As Ruby turned to walk back to her seat, E.V. held her grandmother's arm and immediately noticed a difference. By the closing song, Ruby knew she had been made whole again by the grace of God. She promised the Lord to use every moment for the rest of her earthly life to do good for others.

During E.V.'s next shift at Eastern Lakes, Grams stopped by in her own vehicle. She visited with a number of the residents. Lavender Foley was pleasant but did not remember Ruby Gold, nor did she speak about the space program. After reading Scripture with a married couple, Ruby said she would be leaving but wanted to visit again. The nursing home was still open to visitors, but masks were once again required.

After E.V. said goodbye to her grandmother, she set up a few games in her home wing. Vicky was the nurse on duty. She and E.V. typically got along well. On that day though, Vicky snapped at a nursing assistant and appeared less patient with the residents. E.V. asked Vicky if there was anything she could do for her. The nurse shook her head and apologized. Vicky shared that before leaving that morning, there had been an argument with her partner.

E.V. conveyed that she'd keep Vicky and her husband in her prayers. She had noted that the nurse wore a wedding band. The reaction from the woman was explosive. "I do not have a husband!"

Vicky came back with a vengeance. "Two blob-ectomies were enough to prove I needed no man, Miss Smart Aleck. How dare you assume!"

"Look," E.V. began, "I am sorry for whatever you went through and are still going through."

Vicky's voice softened, "It was just better not to have relations with men." She ranted that women were safer and less toxic for her than males.

She knew not from where it came, but the words arose from Evangeline's soul and sprang out of her mouth, "Where were the daddies?"

"The first was gone by morning. The second, well, let's just say mutual consent was not our chaperone!" Vicky shot back.

E.V. quickly pulled up Bible verses on her phone and calmly stated, "Jeremiah 1:5 says, 'Before I formed you in the womb I knew you, ...' These are words of life, Vicky. Psalm 139:13-14 has been especially soothing for me, '... you knitted me together in my mother's womb. I praise you, for I am wondrously made.'"

A hand went up, "No, no, do not recite Scriptures to me," her voice trailed off. "That's what my parents tried to do."

E.V. sincerely offered, "I am so sorry that you went through that, Vicky. It must have been awful," the dumbfounded woman silently shook her head back and forth, and then opened her mouth to respond, but E.V. continued, "and even worse for the babies who received death sentences."

"You're all alike!" Vicky barked back. "But you're fine if the mother dies in the process or if a rapist gets the electric chair!"

"Life is a gift from the moment of conception until natural death. While convicted rapists, murderers, and drug kingpins on death row have had their sentences commuted, babies rarely receive taxpayers' funding for their legal rights to life," E.V. calmly stated, quietly wondering who was speaking through her and how long it might take for her to be fired from the job.

On the ride home, E.V. received the news bulletin that due to a new pandemic, the country would be going into lockdown on Monday morning. She called Pete and decried the mandate, "No contagion can keep us from God—"

"—Or him from us!" Pete completed her thought.

"Pete, lockdowns were not put in place to help people," E.V. worked to steady her voice. "God instituted some lock-ins like when Noah's family was kept within the Ark for their protection. The Israelites had a lock-in during the tenth plague when the first Passover was instituted and before they moved from Exile into freedom. God shielded baby Moses inside a basket on the Nile River, grown Moses in the desert, and the child Jesus from Herod."

Pete added, "According to 1 Kings 18:4, one hundred of God's prophets were hidden in two groups by Obadiah, to protect them from Jezebel. She was Ahab's wicked wife."

"Tammy showed me Romans 11:5. By God's grace, there has always been a remnant." Then, E.V. prayed, "Be bold, remnant; be bold."

"Amen," uttered Pete.

Chapter Sixteen

LOCKDOWN!

In advance of Ruby's birthday, E.V. took her out to dinner. She decided they would go to a restaurant prior to new government-imposed public restrictions. E.V. also wanted to share and get Grams' take on the conversation that had transpired with Vicky, the nurse. Ruby became serious and introspective after she listened to the account. "Eves, abortion affects many more people than the mother and the child whose life is taken."

"I see," E.V. asserted. They waited for the check so E.V. could pay the bill. She then walked outside with her grandmother and got her situated in the front passenger seat of the car, although Ruby no longer needed help. E.V. moved around to the driver's side and got in.

"Do you still read Bonnie's diary?" Grams questioned.

E.V. started the ignition and shifted the vehicle to reverse, "A little, but I never finished. It became sacred, so for now, I've resealed that tomb."

Ruby spoke with a deliberate urgency, "Eves, I did not recognize the full effect of your mother's procedure, the first time."

E.V. had just backed out of the parking spot and immediately redirected her vehicle forward and within the lines of another space. She put the car in park and then looked over toward her legal guardian. "Grams?"

"Your mother had a second abortion—what I mean to say, Evangeline, is Bonnie had a botched abortion attempt after the first successful one."

E.V.'s voice was barely audible, but the quiet exclamation fully encapsulated her realization, disbelief, and shock, as she breathed, "No!" Minutes passed. Ruby placed her left hand onto E.V.'s right arm. E.V. breathed, "I survived."

"Yes, child, and I thank the Good Lord that you did."

"Grams, please look me in the eyes." The older woman heeded the request. "Did you pay for it?"

Ruby's face was set like stone, "No. We weren't even aware of the second abortion attempt. When Bonnie told G-pa and I that she was still pregnant, we told her we'd do anything to help bring the baby into this world."

"Thank you, Grams." In double-edged silence, they drove home.

After E.V. digested Bonnie's plan to abort her, she prayed. She then began to record ideas in her journal that would later become a sermon. E.V. focused on God's infinite mercy. She prayed that her mother's sins were forgiven. After all, E.V. deduced that the Father's timeline was very different from that of humans. She continued to research Scripture, "For a thousand years in your sight are but as yesterday when it is past, or as a watch in the night." (Psalm 90:4) Next, from 2 Peter 3:8, E.V. copied into her notes, "But do not ignore this one fact, beloved, that with the Lord one day is as a thousand years, and a thousand years as one day."

E.V. could barely keep up with her pen and the words of knowledge that flooded the pages. She expounded on when Roe v. Wade was overturned, sudden desperation filled those who shouted that they were robbed of their rights. E.V.'s ideas flowed, and she was made aware of how the laws had been more than a half century snare of ongoing negation of human rights. Deceptive sales reps working for the enemy used doublespeak to communicate lies that depicted certain death for women in dire straits. The buyers complied, and the losses surpassed tens of millions of lives and the promise of future murders of blameless children. Then, buyers' remorse was not made public after abortions damaged many women who could no longer become pregnant or forgive themselves. The spiritually conflicted spoke from their own selfish, hurting hearts in the name of freedoms. Words were twisted in hopes that the masses would agree that laws were interpreted as rights to healthy lifestyles. Euphemisms meant to distract, pointed to buzzwords like choice and women's bodies but ignored the babies led to slaughter. The same was also described in the Old Testament days of child sacrifice to false idols called baal and molech.

Evangeline often thought about the voice she heard the night she fully accepted Jesus into her own heart. She prayed about it and wondered whether that truly had something to do with her mother or just a daughter's own natural desire to connect with the unknown woman. E.V. finally told herself that everyone needed a legacy. Even outlaws of the wild west left legacies of sorts in their infamy. While her mother was no outlaw, she must have left behind evidence of her traits and talents. E.V. was suddenly emboldened. Bonnie still needed a legacy, thus E.V. penned, "That legacy will come from her daughter, Evangeline Gold."

She dreamed that night and heard the voice of Abba Father, "I have sent my Son. The Greater One lives inside you, Evangeline. It is time for the hard work. My Spirit is within you."

She awoke and with great effort, tried to go back to sleep, to hear his voice, to feel his love. The expectations of God's assignment seemed vague at first but became crystal clear. Schools were shut down again, grocery store hours reduced, and supplies were expected to be limited to a trickle. The government regime threatened that only those vaccinated or chipped would be permitted to vote in person in future elections. Church doors would be locked, thus E.V. clearly understood her calling and what needed to happen.

She was able to focus through the lens of the prophetic that had been instilled within her spirit.

It was Sunday morning. E.V. and Grams got into the car and headed to the church where Dave Marshall was called to shepherd. Nervous tension permeated the air until Pastor Dave promised, with everything in his power, to keep their church open. Millie, Callista, and Frederick showed up as if by some call of solidarity. E.V. had never even known whether any of the three were believers.

After the service, over donuts and fellowship, all six high school friends decided to carpool downtown to a youth gathering that had been planned for months and hadn't yet been canceled. There was still one more day. For weeks, Pete and E.V.'s church had displayed posters for the Christian-based event. There was food, music, and sign-up sheets to encourage young people to become more involved in lifelong commitments to better their church and country. Networking was moving with rapid fire to make as many connections as possible.

During lunch, while listening to the various Christian bands, the students discussed their timelines to complete school. "I cannot believe there's another lockdown!" E.V. exclaimed. She took a breath, "Well, unfortunately I can, and that makes me mad enough to spit!" She recalled Grams using that saying more than once. "To think that they're actually convinced we will be forced to swallow another load of their lies and deceitful trash!" The team of youth discussed whether it would be worth the risk of arrest or getting their loved ones sick. E.V. physically stood up from the park bench where she was sitting. "We won't know if we don't try."

Pete opened his phone and suggested, "Let's pray Psalm 91 right now for protection over our loved ones and ourselves from the snare of the fowler, pestilence, disease, and any other evil."

After, they all said, "Amen," E.V. commented how awesome it was for everyone to attend church together.

"Once Elijah invited us last night," Millie began, "it seemed like a good idea." E.V. smiled at Elijah, and Pete flashed him a thumbs-up sign.

Frederick expanded, "No matter what we do or do not believe."

After the event, many of the young people, including E.V.'s group, walked to a local soup kitchen. Numerous members of the police, who were present for security, fist-bumped the teens. Young people had already assembled. They served others, fed the hungry, and tended to the aged and those imprisoned within their own poor spirits. Frederick looked into Callie's eyes as they were washing pots. "You are most beautiful," he breathed. Pete and E.V. turned aside for the other pair's privacy.

"Thanks, that is the meaning of Callista," the girl grinned, not knowing what else to say.

E.V. recognized, in that moment, that Callista and Millie represented the girls in the dream she had earlier in her senior year. E.V. considered that perhaps, some of her own traits had even been blended into the characters. E.V. was surprised when she realized that Frederick, Pete, and Elijah were a part of that dream, too! There certainly was going to be a God groundbreaking! She felt it. The new lockdown would not imprison any of them, E.V. decided.

As they walked back to their cars, Frederick suggested, "Hey, there's no school tomorrow. Let's meet tonight. I've figured out some more stuff."

Pete reminded everyone, "We have to show up remotely by 8 a.m. Remember the drill?"

They discussed it and decided that the first day might be poorly attended, plus, they'd all be there in some form or another. A unanimous vote was taken for all to meet at E.V.'s place, again. "Because I found the pattern?" she asked with whimsical optimism.

"Not exactly," Frederick was drier than usual.

E.V. called Ruby while others touched base with their families. "Okay," E.V. announced, "my grandmother is ordering food."

After they ate, the teens set up the game. With unsettled resentment, E.V. expressed, "Guys, it's just not feeling much like a game, anymore. It's more like a bad joke that keeps repeating itself with the same punchline. There, I said it. I'm not sure how much more I could offer to this project. The computer glitch is a drag, and I'm already way over this new lockdown."

"Why?" Callie began a bristly cross-examination that indicated she was experiencing her own frustrations. "Do you really think the wool has been pulled over our eyes, E.V.? I get the annoyance and anger over another virus, but maybe the computer program was just a fun advertising piece of a larger puzzle to get people to buy the game title. There might even be future expansion packs planned. With all due respect, E.V., you've repeatedly said that you know very little about online gaming." She sighed, "Anyway, we now have a solid theory for our final math project. Plus, if it was meant to be entertainment, why would they hint at something completely unrelated like your Easter Egg theory?"

"Why?" Elijah suddenly stood up and asked in a sarcastic, cutting tone. All eyes were on him. The smallest one in stature with the largest voice roared, "Arrogance!"

E.V. encouraged him, "Go on, Elijah. Explain more, please."

Elijah shook his head at the rest of the group with exaggerated disbelief. "They either think we're too stupid to figure it out or do not believe there would be any consequences even if they were caught."

The next week, the group met every afternoon when school ended each day. E.V. received a call from Eastern Florida Lakes Veterans Home that due to the epidemic, nonessential employees were not to report to work. Grams told E.V. not to worry about it. She also graciously invited the teens to her home, since it was the only one without younger children who were more susceptible to the new virus.

"What about you, Mrs. Gold?" Pete asked in protection of the older woman.

"Don't you worry about me, young man. I've received some new healing graces." With that, E.V. placed an arm around her grandmother.

The following Sunday, the week after Pastor Dave promised the people that he would keep the church open under the direction of the Lord, Janet noticed two police cars in the parking lot. It was early on a Sunday morning, and Pastor Dave stepped outside to meet the deputies. They asked him to post closed signs on the outside of his church building.

"I cannot do that, officers. The Lord has asked me to keep this church open."

One of the uniformed men spoke in a subdued tone, "We understand your dedication, Reverend." He then whispered, "Just accept the papers and tell us you will put them up."

"I am sorry, gentlemen. I wish I could accommodate you, but my Boss won't permit me to." He glanced upward and then back at the men. "Thank you for understanding."

Just then, E.V. arrived. She watched and was unsure whether to park close to her pastor or away from what was happening. She shut off her car and then drew near to the three men.

Pastor Dave glanced at E.V and evenly stated, "Please, let Janet know," as the handcuffs were closed around his wrists. E.V. was close enough to acknowledge the clicking sound of the metal teeth on the bar of each cuff. One officer reminded David Marshall of his Miranda Rights.

E.V. had trouble finding her voice, "I'll pray for you," she murmured. Pastor Dave had already been placed inside the squad car. E.V. attempted to walk into the church as quickly as she could, but her legs involuntarily trembled with so much force, she felt wobbly.

Pete was setting up music equipment. E.V. embraced him and whispered that she needed to speak to Pete and his mother. They all stepped to the side. When she relayed what had transpired, Pete had obvious concern. Janet nodded and calmly stated that she was not surprised. She assured Pete and E.V. that the Lord had a plan, and all would work out.

The Connors had just arrived. Janet quietly indicated that she needed to speak with them. There were nods and affirmations. Wayne volunteered to preach the service. Tammy busied herself and pulled up appropriate Scriptures on her phone. Janet called a woman from the congregation who was an attorney. The lawyer said that her husband would bring their children to the church, while she went to the local jail. Janet left to meet her incriminated husband. E.V. offered to help watch Pete's younger siblings.

The service went on without a hitch. The musicians were immersed in worship. Wayne asked for the congregation to consider posting bail in their tithe that Sunday. The total amount collected was the exact sum of money needed to the penny.

Many from the church showed up to protest at the police station. They filed complaints that their First Amendment rights were violated by disallowing them the opportunity to assemble and pray. By the time more arrived, Dave Marshall was being released. He urged everyone to remain peaceful and do the will of the Father as Holy Spirit worked in each individual to be a model of Christ.

CHAPTER SEVENTEEN
REVELATION

After online school that Monday, the teens arrived at the Gold's house. Pete and Elijah bought sub sandwiches for everyone. Millie and Callista took care of drinks, and Frederick brought cookies. Ruby was deeply grateful.

The students set up their devices as they had done many times over. "May I?" Callie began. "I've been working on this at home." She opened the laptop and began to show the group her findings. The others looked on as Callista continued, "I learned it utilizes a 256-bit key to encrypt and decrypt data or files," she clarified with a sincere, reconciling smile toward E.V.

"A what?" the familiar questioning look washed over E.V.'s face.

Elijah translated into English for her. "Encryption means locking, so decryption would be unlocking." Elijah nodded his head up and down as the solution unfolded before him. "A different key would be consistently generated for every new session."

Frederick further explained, "Rotational encryption allows messages to be read by substituting one or more symbols like numerals for other characters that remain in fixed positions."

E.V. was excited, "You mean like when we created our own secret codes on paper as kids?"

"Pretty much," Pete verified. "As kids though, we didn't create a new answer key every time we wanted to send a concealed message. But, of course, technology can do that."

E.V. reasoned out loud, "Is that why I was able to assign different variables?" The others all nodded to indicate agreement. "Wow, and I don't even like math!" she grimaced. "That gives us more to submit to our teacher for the final project."

"There's more," Frederick announced. "I've also been toying with the concept of a hidden or cryptographic key that runs through an algorithm to give the impression that the data is disconnected or disjointed, you know, to look like a puzzle with no possible solution."

Millie weighed in, "So, was this just a hoax on the part of the video game company?"

Elijah was quick to answer, "Not a gaming company, Millie, but a pharmaceutical company."

"Sit down, everyone," Frederick advised in a soft tone.

Chills suddenly coursed through E.V.'s veins. For three hours, they were informed and took turns digging, unearthing, and remembering the unfortunate victims. They grieved; some even swore, and they prayed.

A three-way international drug, disease, and human trafficking ring was unveiled. The deception was more complex than anything they could come up with by inputting numerical data into the reality of its calculated production and distribution. The engineered system, once they realized what they were viewing, was live. It was not virtual but being analyzed in real time. There was a constant updating of the values, which was one reason it looked like an error. The teens concluded it had to be something so nefarious that it could be available for large-scale evil but almost unrecognizable when in plain sight. The program's title was decoded and revealed by Elijah as *Pathogen Pathways*.

Elijah stood and remained hyperfocused on the screen. He read, deciphered, and spoke so quickly, that some of the young people simply sat back and listened to his explanations. "The traffickers move viruses, fungi, molds, and bacteria that have been genetically modified to resist eradication. Some have been fully organic, others all chemical, and there were also conglomerates, mixed deep down within the molecular level. They were created to independently affect air, water, soil, plants, and bodily systems of every animal in the kingdom; and that includes humans." He exhaled with force and sat down.

A righteous anger rose up in Pete, "Tunnels of terror for population control that probably used astronomical amounts of taxpayers' money for sinful smuggling rings! We need to pray." Pete took a deep breath to settle himself and led them in a quiet prayer for protection and deliverance from their enemies. Pete sighed, "They easily distributed the digital program to both criminals and kids! May they repent." He paused to collect himself and then continued, "How do the transporters and handlers remain shielded from the toxins?"

Frederick sneered, "They get paid enough not to be protected but are provided with a defense of sorts. Unfortunately, there are probably no safeguards in place for the exploitation of the poor victims or their body parts." Frederick disclosed that he possessed enhanced information from research acquired in Canada that melded with what he gleaned from less than a year of work in the U.S. The young man also shared that lab workers who designed the substances were given a chemical that was abbreviated, MET-L. It temporarily blocked the poisons and was also being tested to provoke metabolically-induced abortions with or without the mother's permission or even her awareness. Callista stood up and quickly left the room. She could be heard vomiting. Millie hesitated and then left the group to check on her friend.

Frederick paused until people stopped moving. He knew what needed to be said about the next part and carefully continued, "MET-L is a metal alloy combined with a polymer of either an organic or synthetic base. The name is an abbreviation of sorts as well as a play on words for the widely used meta, metastasis, and metal, itself. You see, the infection only appears to be diminished by the vaccine, which can also be an infusion or chip placed under the skin. It would theoretically create an antigen to trigger an immune response and thus block the disease but only at the entry site. It was manufactured to shift and affect other regions of the body, like an internal leprosy. Adding further injury through this systemic evil, the design affects and changes DNA structure in cells. The attack is not only spread by close contact but also continues to reinfect the victim from within. Symptoms vary. Long-range complications, if the sick live long enough, are expected to promote blood clots, heart damage, and a variety of cancers. MET-L seems to cause neurological disorders, but it's still early. If there are security leaks of either the poisons or information, the human pack mules will no longer be given the protection of MET-L, which needs frequent boosters."

E.V. gestured with an opened hand, "Who or what caused this, and what about doctors?"

Frederick looked down and shook his head back and forth, "Multifactorial. Remember the first pandemic? Some medical people were on the take. Even now, others still refuse to believe the truth about what happened. And there are those who never wanted to rock the boat or sacrifice their pensions. However, the brave, few docs who fought back have made sacrifices."

E.V. pressed, "Is there a relationship between this evil and the new pandemic, and might it create a black market for MET-L?"

"Both likely but unsubstantiated at the present time," Frederick answered.

"They'll call us co-conspirators," whispered Pete. Then in a louder voice, "Well, there are no coincidences with God. We've all been brought together to spiritually deal with this bioterrorism curse." He stood up to drive the message home. "Furthermore, we are made in the image of God, not in the dysphoric depiction of mutilated DNA chromosomal revisions! My dad has always taught, 'Woe to those who call evil good and good evil.' That's recorded in the Book of the Prophet Isaiah, 5:20." E.V. reached out and placed her hand on Pete's arm in a show of silent support.

Millie returned with Callista, who spoke in a weak and scratchy voice, "I wish it were all just a bad dream."

"How or where did you find out the details, Frederick?" Millie enquired.

"I won't say which web, but in addition to that, I have sources," he offered.

Pete tested, "Frederick, I'm surprised you were allowed to have such information in Canada."

The young man became stern, "I'm not in Canada now, eh?"

As the online game of twisted reality unfolded, E.V. made a connection to the service project at school. It was a symbolic microcosm of what had actually been going on in the world for years. Many actors were involved in making the story look real. Some, like she and Pete, were forced by a bureaucratic leadership to work on the play despite it not being their choice. Sets were created, props moved around, and scenes changed by the playwrights of a syndicate.

The youth left the Gold house feeling completely drained. That night, E.V. had another dream in the sequence. She confessed and asked forgiveness for her own sins. A bright light filled the space where she freely stood, unfettered, amid cinderblocks, iron bars, and other people in chains. Their faces were blurred. Evangeline urged them to break free from the shackles of the enemy and be delivered from bondage. She prayed for them to be covered in the Blood of Christ and accept Jesus as their Lord and Savior. As she preached, chains fell away from people. Light increased from above. It permeated and washed through their souls. She viewed her heart illustration within the dream that featured the beautiful rainbow droplets. For an instant, G-pa Bill, who looked young and handsome, smiled and nodded at E.V. from the exquisite, crystal-clear side of heaven's window. He blew her a kiss. Music poured from the light. In her dream, E.V. noticed that what looked horrible from one side of the glass, looked epic from the opposite perspective.

Multitudes were on a hillside with arms outstretched to the Lord. More light flooded the remnant, who then dispersed God's graces and glory in order to affect others. They could no longer be locked down. It was morning when she woke up, rolled over, and opened her journal. E.V wrote, "Dream over; new life begun."

After E.V. repented for as much as she could recall, God clearly spoke to her heart through journaling, "Evangeline, my Presence will lead you and others into the future. There is no longer any reason to ruminate on your past. Celebrate what you have learned from the ups and downs, and then move away from those times, my Daughter."

E.V. finished her online schooling for the day in one amazing hour. Her energy level was staggering. She messaged her friends. There was work to be done. They agreed on a time to have a computer interface via their devices, because they weren't supposed to leave their homes. Since E.V. had completed her assignments, she outlined the group's remote session. She prayed and knew. Home church was about to be introduced! E.V. finished the announcement with, "Please get the word out, and bring your Bibles on Sunday, everyone! The Word is alive because God is alive!"

Grams was as excited to get started as E.V. was. During the first day of home church, E.V. preached to a small group, "Signs, miracles, and wonders are unfolding. Many see, but many do not. Get ready! Those who cannot see now, will later be counseled by those who saw. Expect weird winds and weather. Crosses have been witnessed in the skies, on mountainsides, and cliffs that meet oceans. Angelic armies, visions, words of knowledge, and more are being recorded worldwide. Eclipses, earthquakes, and strange atmospheric shakings abound. Look, and see while we have access to God's hints. Unexplained, complete darkness in areas is touching upon brilliant light, twenty-four hours a day, in remote places throughout this planet! Those in the darkness cannot cross to light. Those in the light must pray for those in darkness."

There were baptisms in the very same backyard pool where E.V. learned how to swim and used to play with G-pa Bill and Grams. Believers, thirsting to be closer to Jesus, were submerged into the watery death of their old lives and then, emerged reborn. E.V. relied on her mentor, Tammy Connor, as a spiritual sounding board. Music and art had filled Evangeline in her past. Now, Jesus filled her.

Graduation day had finally arrived the following week. The high school held the event outdoors on a football field to reduce the chance of infections. Friends from the gaming group were there. Frederick, as a foreign exchange student, was ineligible to receive a diploma in the state of Florida, so he sat in the stands. During the drive home, E.V. told Ruby she wanted to begin classes at the local community college in the fall. She had decided, "I'd like to get my prerequisites out of the way and then go to nursing school. Spending time with cool people at Eastern Florida Lakes has been life-changing for me, Grams."

"You'll make a fantastic nurse, Eves. You know, Bonnie spoke of going to nursing school."

E.V. nodded, "Yeah, I read it in her diary."

That night, the teen and her grandmother spoke about how different the lockdown felt the second time around. Ruby agreed, "Many folks don't seem to be paying much mind to it."

"True, but Pastor Dave was arrested for that!" E.V. interjected. "And here we are, still meeting every Sunday. I don't trust them at all, Grams. They're planning to come against us with something new. We need to lift our voices in prayer and rebuke such moves."

Two days later, the power grid partially went down. Sporadic electricity showed itself with flickering lights, at best, during low-usage hours. No one completely understood the depth or breadth of what was happening. There were widespread phone outages as well. "No need to be watching the news we don't trust, anyway," E.V. chided Grams and her friends.

Internet conductivity vacillated between being barely detectable and completely devoid of service. Sheriff's vehicles drove through their town announcing, "All public facilities are closed due to an epidemic. Please, stay home. Violators will be prosecuted."

Referring to the lack of electricity, E.V. proclaimed on a Sunday afternoon at their growing church meeting, "That's just one more attempt by the loser enemy!" Folks arrived in small groups and parked away from E.V.'s house and walked so as not to expose the large gatherings. Word got out, and people showed up. They began earlier in the day to have more daylight. "God has already won! The enemy is done!" E.V. declared to the growing crowd.

The large group began to chant over and over again, "God has won! The enemy's done! God has won! The enemy's done!"

Finally, E.V. was able to continue. "We will still trust and believe. Even with no internet and little lighting, just look at how many people are here. Praise the Lord! Let's all proclaim James 4:7, 'Submit yourselves therefore to God. Resist the devil and he will flee from you.' No contagion can keep us from God!" cried E.V. "We know from Isaiah 54:17, that 'no weapon formed against us shall prosper.'" She held up her grandfather's Bible and continued, "Romans 10:17 tells us, 'So faith comes from what is heard, and what is heard comes by the preaching of Christ.'"

"Come on!" shouted Tammy Connor. "You preach it, girl!" The people raised their hands in the air, lifted their voices in Hallelujahs, and applauded the Lord.

The students continued to meet at Ruby's house, since it was in the most rural setting of all the group. The young adults had been ready and waiting for a power outage. During one of their potluck meals, Ruby asked the young people how they knew. Elijah simply pointed to his head and suggested, "You have to think like a bad guy, Miss Ruby."

Elijah already had the local server on his laptop. He and his father had previously fashioned a metal device to transmit and receive radio waves that created a frequency to bounce off a nearby cell tower that would function as a massive antenna to share data. Thus, one could type a message that could be sent when the power was back on, even if temporary.

The students worked to create their own chat room that utilized a single text document and would have its own time stamp. In that way, messages could be sent and received when the power came on for small intervals, thus maintaining communication without solid phone or internet connections. The group reasoned that whoever or whatever controlled the rationed electricity would allow it to come back in small increments to avoid all out protests and chaos.

The Connors had the know-how to store information on their local server that created an intranet just for their immediate group. It used frequencies to treat an antenna as a router for their own private message usage. Elijah explained how his dad taught him that their own frequency would be slow and permeating, thus enabling communication. Elijah also learned that the frequency would still need to be higher than that used by radios, so others wouldn't discover it.

That was Ruby's cue to jump aboard. She had skills in radio communications as part of her space mission training. Frederick offered to make a cantenna from an empty metallic-lined, cylindrical potato chips' cardboard container. E.V. was certain Frederick had invented the term until he explained it. He rigged an old router to the homemade antenna and the weak contraption became a wireless receiver with a boost. Frederick commented that it wasn't a perfect solution but still better than having no digital messaging capability. Everyone thanked him. Frederick expressed his appreciation to all of them for having accepted him as part of their inner circle. A diverse group of youths had come together for a united purpose.

Chapter Eighteen
REVIVAL

The Golds continued to celebrate home church on their property. The youth were present. The elderly arrived. Children proclaimed the name of Christ Jesus and prophesied. They came with their parents and extended family. Worshippers carried lawn chairs and blankets to sit on. People spilled past the yard. Pastor Dave brought more anointed ones to pray and preach. Musicians began to attend. The services often continued into the early morning hours with signs such as deliverance and healings. Crutches and wheelchairs were left leaning against Ruby's garage.

Many carried Bibles and journals. After a few weeks, a group of youth with one elderly lady arrived with strings of beads dangling from their hands. E.V. noticed the individuals when she turned her head to acknowledge her estranged friend, Destiny. E.V. shrugged as the old woman and the young people simultaneously recited the same words aloud. Destiny stepped nearer to E.V. and quietly remarked that the group was praying the Rosary. E.V. had heard about that in World Religions class. "E.V.," Destiny continued, "the prayers come from Scripture."

E.V. whispered, and her eyes narrowed, "I heard they pray to Jesus's mother, Mary."

"Actually, they ask her, a human saint in heaven, to pray for us, just as we would ask a friend or relative to pray for us. I know about that, because my grandmother was Catholic."

E.V. raised her eyebrows, then nodded. The old woman looked up and walked directly to E.V. She pressed an oval medal into Evangeline's hand. E.V. studied the lady with a quizzical expression. The woman with the prayer beads gently offered, "It's a miraculous medal."

"Like a charm?" E.V. whispered.

"No, not at all; it's a sacramental. The image was given in a vision, to a young woman in France, almost two hundred years ago. It's been blessed, and the properties are divine. Put it on, and wear it. Ask Jesus to teach you more. Test the spirit. And, thank you for discerning that the Lord has been calling us." The lady smiled and returned to prayer with her group.

Something moved E.V. to clip the piece of metal to the cross on her bracelet from Pete, which she always wore. It was a tangible reminder of just how much God was with her. The healing of her arms and heart were gifts from Jesus. E.V. made her way through the crowd and welcomed worshippers. People carried prayer cards, devotionals, prayer tracts, and shofars made from rams' horns, which some blew loudly during the service and sounded like trumpet blasts.

Emma and Nick showed up. They asked for Evangeline's forgiveness, and she asked for theirs. E.V. was compelled to speak, "The challenge is not to treat others as they mistreat us but to pray past our temptations, so we may share the graces and forgiveness of Christ."

Nick mentioned that the couple had been attending Emma's LDS church. E.V. stared, unsure. "Mormons," Emma declared. "We have a deep love for Heavenly Father. Our church doors are locked at the moment."

E.V. welcomed them, along with a few self-proclaimed Messianic Jews, and many from other Christian denominations. "This is big," E.V. whispered to herself as she surveyed the area.

Every prayer meeting brought even more precious people. E.V. reintroduced herself to each of the original sidewalk girls, Kelly, Becca, and Meagan. Shaking each young woman's hand, E.V. warmly added, "Welcome! God loves you, and he is here. Please accept my apologies for anything I've ever done that hurt you."

There were more young people than in the earlier meetings. The tatted and pierced led the way. They were passionate individuals who were on fire for the Lord! Many had become so strong in their faith that their conversion stories became God's glory stories and wrenched others away from darkness and toward the light of Christ.

Muslims, Hindus, Buddhists, self-proclaimed Free Masons, Atheists, and Agnostics trickled in. One evening, Nick, a new Christian, pointed and shouted, "Hey, they can't be here!"

His words and demeanor suddenly drew E.V. back to the school festival. She raised both hands high in the air. Others followed, and the crowd quieted. "We are all sinners in need of repentance. My sisters and brothers, if we promote division here and now, then the enemy has won this round. Let's pray Ephesians 6:10-20, to put on the whole armor of God for strength and protection; Psalm 23 for peace; and Psalm 91 against pestilence, darkness, and troubles. Please, open your Bibles, and share with those who do not have theirs."

During the worship and praise music, a prophetic man from Pastor Dave's church approached E.V. and privately shared that her progeny would disciple others during the upcoming era of peace. E.V. took it all in and thanked him for the word of knowledge. E.V. then remarked that she sensed the man had a word for the entire group. He nodded, took hold of the portable microphone, and began to address the crowd with words from Ephesians 4:11-13. "The gifts of the five-fold are 'to equip the saints for the work of ministry, for building up the body of Christ, until we all attain to the unity of faith ...'"

That which Evangeline heard resonated within, but her attention was quickly drawn to a pair of uniformed individuals from the sheriff's department. They wound their way through the yard. E.V recognized the woman deputy who had come to the Gold's door when E.V. called for a welfare check on Nick. The other had been the officer who interviewed her at school when she reported the odd events at the Christian Ministry booth during the festival.

They came to speak with Frederick, and E.V. overheard it all. The young man vouched that he was legally in the U.S. as a foreign exchange student from Canada. He politely answered their questions and firmly insisted he was not a spy. Frederick admitted that he entered the yard that day to come to the Lord. What happened next was miraculous. Every individual at the meeting was bathed in God's glory, including law enforcement. No one saw Frederick slip away.

When the Golds' home church began to overflow into the streets of their neighborhood, Pastor Dave invited the worshippers to meet with lawn chairs the following Sunday in the large parking lot of his locked church. That Sunday, he preached the Word about prodigals coming home. Dave, a pastor, husband, and father suddenly looked up. Janet stood up amidst the outdoor congregation. Her hands covered her face and mouth. Dave paused as his eyes focused on a female in her early twenties, "Welcome home, Dawn," her father offered. Janet stepped forward and threw her arms around their estranged daughter. Pete never mentioned where his older sister was, but she had returned to the flock, like so many others. Evangeline had a strong knowing that she and the young woman would become best of friends as she continued to play music with the worship team.

When summer temperatures and rain made meeting outdoors a challenge, worship times were changed to start closer to sundown. Then, in a sudden bold move, Pastor Dave simply unlocked the church doors and bade everyone inside. Although the electricity was intermittent, it was more comfortable indoors. On one Sunday evening, members from the sheriff's department showed up. They handed Dave Marshall a notice. He invoked a blessing and invited them to the service. The two young officers looked at the hundreds of people gathered, turned back to their vehicles, and drove away.

Revival without restoration would be incomplete. In the weeks and months to come, people refused to remain in lockdown the second time around. They peacefully poured into the streets, defying mandates. Hours before primary elections, the unconstitutional ruling that only allowed in-person voting for the vaccinated was struck down. A magnificent promise of fair and just leaders had emerged. Folks returned to work and produced goods and provided services. When baffled representatives from three-letter agencies showed up at the doors of Christians and patriots to "simply ask for information," the officials were politely turned away, empty-handed. Whistleblowers exposed individuals from departments that had been accustomed to overreach for their own profit and power. The accused and indicted globalists, who never imagined they'd be caught, turned against each another in attempts to gain favor in the courtrooms for their own plea deals.

Courts that had been inundated with corruption were overtaken by the justice of God. Poor souls, unlawfully imprisoned for doing no wrong, were released. Included in the thousands of people who had been stripped of their rights were Christians, patriots, farmers, young parents, and not-so-young but innocent grandparents. Bank accounts that had been encroached upon, now overflowed with a variety of currencies. The rich and evil, who had abused their powerful investments, lost it all. Human trafficking and *Pathogen Pathways* crumbled. The innocent ones were rescued. Prior unbelievers attested, beyond any doubt, that the move of God's hand was upon the world.

Positive outcomes were strengthened by a remnant of steadfast youth who prayed, preached, and interceded for peace in all lands. Many repented publicly and pleaded for mercy and forgiveness of the sins in their nations. Darkness gave way to light that permeated and shone through lifelong as well as new believers. There was a harvest of souls that neither humans nor principalities could suppress. God was on the move and showed himself, which resulted in an incredible outpouring of love on his people.

Once energy sources were powered back up, copious surprises teemed across the globe. Home churches and an ongoing fire of revival had spread across the world from small villages to big cities. Numerous prayer services and meetings had no defined conclusions. Speakers from the five-fold ministry alternated shifts with musicians. Churches that stayed open, bringing the Word of God to the hearts of his people during the lockdown, remained open for twenty-four hours, every day. Some of those had been traditional churches while others carried the stamp of nondenominational. A large number of megachurches that many had once flocked to, ended up closing their doors for good. The universal Church on earth was alive and took on a meaning that encompassed more than its physical locale. Numerous church buildings that housed feckless, fearful leaders had kept their doors locked and never reopened.

Less than a year prior, universities shut down their campuses because of rioting and chaos caused by influencers and infiltrators. The causes were similar to what had occurred at E.V.'s high school campus but on a much larger scale. No one was sure whether it was connected to the new pandemic. Astute members of society asked whether forces involved in the rioting in U.S. cities that preceded the first pandemic should be studied and compared to the more recent turmoil. Those who developed such treasonous plans needed to pay for their crimes of terror and licentiousness.

When schools went back in session, one thing students, staff, and administrators were sure of was the winding up of Holy Spirit's move. God was invited into both public and private institutions. Social issues and labels that had been meant to divide people were no longer necessary. God was both, the concentrated cause as well as the unifying effect. There was no longer a call for wars or rumors of war. Christ the King was in charge, so the entity out to steal, kill, and destroy was squelched. The tempter had overplayed its hand

and was out of a job. God graced the planet and released his glory upon everyone.

The young people in E.V.'s closest circle of friends quietly credited Frederick. He secured significant details about the depraved design of *Pathogen Pathways* and conveyed the message through trusted channels. In a single chat that arrived from Frederick after he had vanished, they learned more about him. He was in the States on assignment from a private Canadian group to uncover what he couldn't do in his own home country. Frederick was actually a highly intelligent man of twenty-two, who looked like a high school senior. He was in the U.S. as part of a study to survey young Americans who might stand against a globalist government. In that message, Frederick called himself a research assistant. The teens didn't actually know whether exposing the destructive scheme was part of Frederick's duties but remembered that he mentioned having sources.

E.V. recalled overhearing the deputies in her yard ask Frederick if he had identified any suspicious individuals who might turn against the authorities. The young man reported that he had not. When the group of friends tossed around possible explanations for why Frederick had trusted them, E.V. offered, "Frederick needed to share the truth with a select few, just in case something happened to him. Maybe it wasn't us he trusted but through us, came to know and trust the Lord." Even after communications were reinstated for most, the group members were unable to contact Frederick.

Numerous actors from multi-layered, evil operations were jailed. Hostages of all ages were set free. The majority of people who had been overcome and overjoyed by revival knew nothing about the justice that was being served. People who allowed themselves to be molded in the hands of God, the Potter, no longer cried out for vengeance but for love. Those disheartened and confused by the aftershocks of the shaking were comforted and guided by others.

Although a viral contagion had once again crept into their lives, it quickly vanished. Many prayed, and prayers were answered regarding worldwide events. Pastor Dave preached Zechariah 2:8-9 as one of numerous Bible verses where enemies were warned not to touch Israel, the apple of the eye of the Lord of Hosts. The United States had been founded upon principles that encompassed a love for the Lord. When those two nations returned to the balance of powers, other nations also had peace, some for the first time, ever. Numerous politicians stepped down. Crooked world leaders disappeared. Some died. Some retired. Some resigned. The guilty were jailed with harsh but just sentences.

True shepherds, selected by citizens of the constitutional republic of the U.S.A., were installed to watch over and care for their flocks. The voice of the people had won, because they spoke the Word of God. Peace reigned. It took a number of years for all the players of the deep state to be exposed, but they were rendered impotent by the prayers and actions of upright people of God.

One evening, E.V. had a short, yet powerful dream. She approached the throne room of God. Due to the immense presence and anointing of the Father, she fell facedown. Trembling, it took everything from within her to ask, "Why, Abba, has this revival been initiated by the youth?"

She sensed the Father nod, although his light was too bright to look upon. Even without hearing his voice, Evangeline knew what Father God was saying. "Over time, I have given mature men and women multiple opportunities for such a harvest of souls. Some have obeyed. Now is the time for the most powerful revival of all to save souls and fend off the wicked. Today's youth will carry and send forth their children into a very different world, Daughter Evangeline. Your progeny will disciple others during the upcoming era of peace."

When she awoke, E.V. immediately transcribed the experience into her journal. That was when she recognized the fuller meaning of the dream from early in that school year. Jesus had stood on the bridge and empowered his children by his spirit. E.V. rapidly scribbled out the message. The bridge represented God, himself. Jesus was there, bridging any gaps so all people could be included. A new era of believers lovingly embraced those who had been old believers, no-longer believers, and non-believers.

All charges against Pastor David Marshall were dropped. His church services became so crowded that outdoor seating was installed. The congregation suggested their pastor find or construct a larger building. Instead, the church hired additional ministers to cover many more services so the church would still project a spirit of warmth through immediacy. The pastor's son, Peter, attended business school and dated a certain nursing student, Evangeline Gold.

One day, E.V. was playing her violin during an outdoor service. Church was no longer exclusively confined to Sunday mornings. There were additional times for worship, fellowship, and Bible study classes for learners of all ages. E.V. happened to look over at her grandmother, who was seated with young people. Ruby was not the only one who remained young at heart, and she was fully dedicated to the Lord within her core.

Ruby sat in the outdoor pavilion with love in her eyes. She wore a new dress and a stylish hat to keep the sun off her face. E.V. eyed her grandmother with admiration. She refused to allow herself to pity the aging woman of God. E.V. knew that when it would be Ruby's time, Jesus would come for her with G-pa Bill close by. Together, their prayers among the cloud of witnesses would be a force to be reckoned with. E.V. smiled as she shook her head to drive away any tears. She never thought that her grandfather would be out of her existence so quickly, but Grams had become more than a fixture in E.V.'s own life. She was not only a major part of the young woman's formation but someone E.V. loved and respected.

While E.V. fixed her eyes on Ruby, she unexpectedly saw through the present and clearly into the future. In the vision, Grams appeared to be an old, small, frail lady. Ruby Gold was almost completely blind, yet she declared aloud that the future never looked brighter nor had she ever seen more clearly. The smell of fresh-cut grass evoked memories of a carefree childhood. Summer permeated the air. Of course, grass grew all year in Florida. Nevertheless, Evangeline was sure that the trimming of summer grass would always bring about its own fond memories along with sweet new growth.

The End

Milton Keynes UK
Ingram Content Group UK Ltd.
UKHW021930281024
450365UK00017B/1016

9 798868 503993